Margaret Millar was born in ⟨...⟩ ⟨...⟩ nd educated at the Kitchener Colle⟨...⟩ ⟨...⟩ and ⟨...⟩ University of Toronto. In 1938 she married Kenneth Millar. better known under his pen name of Ross Macdonald, and for over forty years they enjoyed a unique relationship as a husband and wife who successfully pursued writing careers.

She published her first novel. *The Invisible Worm,* in 1941. Now, almost five decades later, she is busily writing her twenty-sixth work of fiction. During that time she has established herself as one of the great practitioners in the field of mystery and psychological suspense. Her work has been translated into more than a dozen foreign languages, appeared in twenty-seven paperback editions and has been selected seventeen times by book clubs. She received an Edgar Award for the Best Mystery of the year with her classic *Beast In View*; and two of her other novels, *The Fiend* and *How Like an Angel*, were runners-up for that award. She is past President of the Mystery Writers of America, and in 1983 she received that organization's most prestigious honor, the Grand Master Award, for lifetime achievement.

Novels by **MARGARET MILLAR**
available in Crime Classics ® editions:

AN AIR THAT KILLS
ASK FOR ME TOMORROW
BANSHEE
BEAST IN VIEW
BEYOND THIS POINT ARE MONSTERS
THE CANNIBAL HEART
THE FIEND
FIRE WILL FREEZE
HOW LIKE AN ANGEL
THE IRON GATES
THE LISTENING WALLS
MERMAID
THE MURDER OF MIRANDA
ROSE'S LAST SUMMER
SPIDER WEBS
A STRANGER IN MY GRAVE
VANISH IN AN INSTANT
WALL OF EYES

MARGARET MILLAR

MERMAID

LIBRARY OF CRIME CLASSICS®

MISTER E'S℠

INTERNATIONAL POLYGONICS, LTD.
NEW YORK CITY

Library of Congress Card Catalog # 91-73852
ISBN 1-55882-114-7

Printed and manufactured in the United States of America.
First IPL printing October 1991.

10 9 8 7 6 5 4 3 2 1

to Eleanor McKay Van Cott

CONTENTS

1

CHILD

1

The girl was conspicuous even before she entered the office. It was a windy day and everything was in motion except her face. Her coat beat against her legs like captive wings and her long fair hair seemed to be trying to tie itself into knots. The sign above the door, SMEDLER, DOWNS, CASTLEBERG, MACFEE, POWELL, ATTORNEYS AT LAW, twisted and turned as if the partners were struggling among themselves.

Charity Nelson, Mr. Smedler's private secretary, was taking the receptionist's place during the lunch hour because she herself was on a diet and didn't want to see or think of food.

The front door opened and the wind pushed the girl into the office. She looked surprised at what had happened. She was very thin, which made Charity think about food and sent nasty little pains up and down and around her stomach.

She said irritably, "What can I do for you?"

"I like the little cage."

"Little cage?"

"The one outside . . . the one at the back."

"That's Mr. Smedler's own elevator. It leads to his private office."

"Do you think he'd give me a ride in it?"

"No."

"Not even one?"

"Only if you were a client."

The girl didn't look like a client, at least not the kind who paid. She was quite pretty, with high cheekbones and large brown eyes as bright and expressionless as glass.

"Do you wish to see Mr. Smedler?" Charity said.

"I don't know."

She took a seat at the corner window and picked up a magazine. It lay on her lap unopened and, Charity noticed, upside down.

"Are you sure you came to the right office?" Charity said.

"Yes, I took a taxi. The driver knew just where to go."

"I didn't mean how did you get here. I meant did you have a specific reason for coming. You realize this is a law firm."

"I'm bothering you, aren't I? My brother Hilton is always telling me I mustn't bother people, but how can I help it if I don't know what bothers them?"

"Would you care to make an appointment with one of our attorneys?"

"I think I'll just sit here for a while and look around."

"Everyone's out to lunch."

"I don't mind," the girl said. "I'm not in a hurry."

At 1:25 they began returning to the office: two typists, a file clerk, Mr. MacFee with a client, Mr. Powell and his secretary, a junior member of the firm and the receptionist, who looked, Charity noted bitterly, well-fed and contented.

The girl showed her first sign of excitement. She rose suddenly, dropping the magazine on the floor.

"That's him," she said. "He's who I want to see, the one wearing the glasses. He has a nice face. What's his name?"

"Tom Aragon. What's yours?"

"Cleo."

"Cleo what?"

"The same as my brother Hilton's. Jasper, Cleo Jasper. It's awfully ugly, don't you think?"

"I'll check and see if Mr. Aragon will have time to talk to you." She told Aragon on the intercom: "Some chick is waiting to see you because you have a nice face. Can you buy that?"

"Sure. Send her in."

"Better come out and get her, junior. She looks like she couldn't find her way out of a wet paper bag."

Aragon shared an office with another junior member of the firm. It was furnished as if no clients were expected, and in fact few came. Aragon's duties were mostly confined to legwork for the senior lawyers, especially Smedler, whose cases often involved rich women. Cleo Jasper wasn't yet a woman and she didn't look rich. The straight-backed chair she sat down on seemed to suit her better than the overstuffed leather surrounding Smedler. Her clothes were oddly childish, a navy-blue jumper over a white blouse, white knee socks and shoes that looked like the Mary Janes of another era. She wasn't carrying a handbag, but one of the pockets of her jumper bulged as though it contained a coin purse.

"What can I do for you, Miss Jasper?"

"I've never been to a lawyer before. You have a nice face —that's why I picked you."

"I suppose it's as good a reason as any other," Aragon said. "Why do you need a lawyer?"

"I want to find out my rights. I have a new friend. He says I have some rights."

"Who claims you don't?"

"Nobody exactly. Except that I never get to do what I want to do, what other people do."

"Like what?"

"Vote. Not that I specially want to vote, not knowing anything about Presidents and things, but I didn't even know I could."

"How old are you?"

"Twenty-two. My new friend says I could have voted four years ago and nobody even told me."

"Wasn't the subject brought up in school?"

"I can't remember. I have foggy times. Hilton says voting is just for responsible people, who don't have foggy times."

"Are you an American citizen?"

"I was born right here in Santa Felicia." The girl frowned. "It was a terrible occasion. Hilton and his wife, Frieda, often talk about how it was such a terrible occasion."

"Why?"

"My mother died. She was too old to have a baby but she had one anyway and I'm it. Hilton says she almost got into the record book because she was forty-eight. Hilton was already grown up and married when I was born. But I didn't go to stay with him and Frieda until I was eight. I lived with my grandmother before that. She was very nice, only she died. Hilton says she wore herself out worrying over me. She left me a lot of money. I never get to use it, though."

"Why not?"

"I'm exceptional."

"I see."

"Well, are you surprised or aren't you?"

"Not particularly. All people are exceptional in one way or another."

"You don't understand. I'm . . . My new friend has lots

of fun ways of saying it, like I have a few marbles missing or I've only got one oar in the water or I'm not playing with a full deck. It sounds better like that than spelling it right out that I'm . . . you know, retarded."

He was, in fact, surprised. She had none of the Down's syndrome physical features and she spoke well, expressing herself quite clearly. She even wanted to vote. Whether or not she was simply echoing the ideas of her new friend, it seemed an unusual desire on the part of a retarded girl.

Not girl, he thought. She was a woman of twenty-two. That's where the retardation was more obvious. If she'd claimed to be fourteen or fifteen he would have believed her.

"Can you read and write?"

"Some. Not very much."

"What about your new friend? Does he read and write very well?"

"Oh, gosh yes. He's one of the . . ." She slapped her left hand over her mouth so quickly and decisively it must have hurt her. "I'm not supposed to talk about him to anyone."

"Why not?"

"It would spoil things. He's my only friend except for the gardener and his dog, Zia. Zia is a basset hound. Do you like basset hounds?"

"Yes."

"I just love them."

"Getting back to your new friend . . ."

"No. No, I really mustn't."

"All right. We'll talk about the voting. I believe the only requirements are that you be an American citizen, at least eighteen years old, not on parole or confined to a mental institution and that you sign an affidavit to that effect. You are, of course, expected to be able to read the affidavit before signing."

17

"I could practice ahead of time, couldn't I?"

"Of course."

Her lips began to move as though she was already practicing in silence. She had a small, well-shaped mouth with prominent ridges between the upper lip and the nose. According to old wives' tales, when this area was clearly defined it indicated strength of character. Aragon looked at the timid, underdeveloped girl in front of him and decided the old wives must have been wrong.

She said finally, "Tell me about my other rights."

"Which ones?"

"Suppose I just wanted to get on a bus and go somewhere . . . oh, somewhere like Chicago. Could I do that?"

"It depends on whether you have sufficient funds and whether you feel capable of looking after yourself in a large city. It would be a good idea to talk it over first with your brother and his wife."

"No way."

"Why not?"

"They wouldn't let me go. I've never been anyplace except once last Easter on a boat. Me and some of the other students at Holbrook were taken on a cruise to Catalina on Donny Whitfield's father's yacht."

Holbrook Hall was known throughout Southern California as a school for the troubled and troubling offspring of the very wealthy. In the more expensive magazines it was advertised as "a facility designed to meet the special needs of exceptional teenagers and young adults."

"How long have you been at Holbrook Hall, Cleo?"

She blushed very faintly. "You called me Cleo. That's nice. It's friendly, you know."

"How long?"

"Forever."

"Come on, Cleo."

"A year, maybe longer. I always had a governess before that. Also Hilton and Frieda gave me lessons in things. He's really smart and she used to be a schoolteacher. Ted goes to college. He's their son. He drinks and smokes pot and . . . well, lots of things like that. Imagine him being my nephew and he's only a year younger than I am. He tells everybody I'm a half-wit that his parents found in an orphanage."

"So you want to get away from Ted and your brother and sister-in-law."

"Mainly I only want to know my rights."

"Is there money available to you?"

"I have charge cards. But if I used any of them to do something Hilton disapproved of he would probably cancel them. At least that's what my new friend says."

"Your new friend seems to have quite a few opinions about your affairs."

"Oh my, yes. Some I don't understand. Like he says we are all in cages and we must break out of them. I thought if I could get inside the cage that goes up and down your building and then out by myself again I would sort of understand what he's talking about."

"Why not ask him?"

"I'm supposed to try and figure things out by myself. He says I'm not as dumb as I act. I don't understand that part either and I try. I try real, real hard."

"I'm sure you do," Aragon said. Cleo's new friend, whatever his motive, was feeding her stuff she couldn't digest. "What else does your friend advise you to do?"

"He thinks I should take some money from my savings account and spend it on whatever I want, without Hilton's permission."

"Could you do that?"

"I guess. If I wasn't scared."

"Does your friend ever bring up the subject of borrowing any of this money?"

"Oh, no. He hates money. He says it's rotten, only that's not the word he used."

" 'The love of money is the root of all evil.' Is that what he said?"

"Why, yes." She looked pleased. "So you know him too."

"No. We've both read some of the same books. The quotation is from the Bible."

"Is that what the Bible really says about money?"

"One of the things."

"Then I suppose it's true. It's funny, though, because Hilton is very Christian, yet he works all the time to make more of it."

"People often do."

"Hilton quotes the Bible quite a bit. Ted says it's a bunch of—he used a bad word. Ted knows more bad words than anyone in the world except Donny Whitfield at school. Donny talks so dirty hardly anybody can understand him. He's fat. On our free afternoons from school we each get five dollars to spend and Donny spends his all on ice cream. His afternoons are never really free, he has to have a counselor with him every minute to keep him out of trouble. He's a bad boy. Why are there good boys and bad boys?"

"No one can answer that, Cleo."

"You'd think if God was going to the trouble of making boys in the first place he'd just make good ones."

Charity Nelson, Mr. Smedler's secretary, stuck her head in the door. When she saw that the girl was still there she raised her eyebrows until they almost disappeared under her orange wig.

"Mr. Smedler wants to see you, junior."

"Tell him I have a client."

"I told him. He didn't believe me."

"Tell him again."

"You're playing with fire, junior. Smedler had a big weekend."

When Charity closed the door again the girl said, "That woman doesn't like me."

"Miss Nelson doesn't like many people."

"I'd better leave now." She glanced uneasily at the door as if she were afraid Charity might be hiding behind it. "I took too much of your time already."

"Fifteen minutes."

"Hilton says every second counts. He says time and tide wait for no man, whatever that means. It must mean something or Hilton wouldn't say it."

"What brought you to this office in the first place?"

"Nothing. I mean I pass here every day on my way to Holbrook Hall. Frieda and Hilton drive me mostly but sometimes Ted when he's home from college. That's scary but sort of fun too. Anyway, that's how I saw the little cage moving up and down and wanted a ride in it and . . . and. . . ."

She had begun to stammer and he couldn't understand her words. He waited quietly until she calmed down. He didn't know what had excited her, all the talking she'd done or memories of riding scarily with Ted or something deeper and inexplicable.

She pressed her fists against the sides of her mouth as if to steady it. "Also I wanted to see a lawyer about my rights. I thought if I came here I'd get to ride in the little cage."

"Sorry. That's not possible today."

"Some other time?"

"Maybe."

"Maybe's never happen," she said. "Not the nice ones anyway."

"This one will."

She stood up and removed the coin purse from her pocket. "I'll pay you now." She emptied the contents of the purse on his desk: three one-dollar bills, two quarters and a nickel. "I hope this is enough. I had to pay the taxi to bring me here and this is all that's left of my free-afternoon money."

"Let's make the charge one dollar. This is your first visit and I haven't helped you very much."

"You tried," she said softly. "And you have a nice face."

"Shall I call you a taxi?"

"No, I can walk. I think I'll go to the museum. The staff likes us to go to the museum on free days. They think we're learning something. How far is it from here?"

"About a mile and a half. Do you know the way?"

"Oh sure. I've been there millions of times. . . ."

He watched from the window as she left the building. The museum was due north. She walked rapidly and confidently south.

2

The table was long and dark walnut, carved in the intricate Georgian style and designed for an elegant English dining room. But Hilton sat at the head of it as though he were a captain instructing his crew on how to maneuver through stormy seas, which to Hilton meant taxes, Democrats, inflation, undercooked lamb and bad manners.

The crew wasn't paying much attention. His wife, Frieda, had brought a copy of *TV Guide* to the table and was surveying the evening's listings. She was a pretty woman given to fat and to peevish little smiles when she was annoyed and didn't want to admit it. They appeared frequently during mealtime when she was struck by the gross unfairness of Hilton being able to eat everything in sight and never gain an ounce, while she couldn't even walk past a chocolate éclair without putting on a pound or two.

The rest of the crew was equally inattentive. Lisa, the college student who served dinner every night because the cook refused to work after seven o'clock, moved rhythmically in and out and around and about as if she had an invisible radio stuck in her ear. Her skintight jeans and T-shirt were partly hidden by an embroidered white bib apron, the closest thing to a uniform that Frieda could coax her into wearing. She was the same age as Cleo but the two seldom had any personal communication except for occasional shrugs and eye rollings when Hilton was being particularly boring.

Cleo sat with her left hand propping up her head, her eyes fixed on the plate in front of her.

Frieda had come to depend on television for company. Hilton was often away on business, and even when he was at home the conversation was kept on Cleo's level so Cleo wouldn't feel excluded. It was Frieda herself who felt excluded.

"Please remove your elbow from the table, Cleo," Hilton said. "And eat your soup like a good girl."

"I can't. It's got funny things in it like shells."

"They *are* shells. It's bouillabaisse."

"And bones too."

"Well?"

"The gardener won't even give his dog bones. He says they might make holes in his bowels."

"I don't consider this a suitable subject for dinner conversation. Now eat your soup. Cook makes excellent bouillabaisse. Waste not, want not."

"Oh, for heaven's sake," Frieda said. "Don't eat the soup if you don't like it. . . . Now tell us what you did today."

"I went to the museum."

"You were gone all afternoon."

"I saw lots and lots of pictures."

"Did you meet anyone?"

"There were lots and lots of people."

"I meant, did you talk to anyone?"

"One person."

"Was it a man or a woman?"

"A man."

"Cleo, dear, we're not trying to pry," Hilton said. "But what did you and this man talk about?"

"I asked him where the ladies' room was. And he told me, and then he said, 'Have a nice day,' so I did."

There was a brief silence, then Hilton's voice sounding worried: "I thought the museum was closed on Mondays."

The girl sat mute and pale, staring down at the bones and shells in front of her until Lisa came to take them away.

A twitch appeared at the corner of Hilton's right eye, moving the lid like an evil little wink. "Of course you know how important it is to tell the truth, don't you, Cleo?"

"I went to the museum. There were lots and lots of pictures. I saw lots and lots of people. . . ."

"I care about you very deeply, Cleo. Your welfare was entrusted to me. I have to know where you go and what company you keep."

"I go to Holbrook Hall. I have lots of company at Holbrook Hall."

"Leave the girl alone for now," Frieda said sharply.

"Obviously this is one of her foggy times. We can't expect her to behave like a normal person."

"I am exceptional," Cleo said.

"Certainly you are, dear. And it's not your fault you're different. Everyone's different. Look at Lisa. She's different from other people."

"In what way?" Lisa said, putting the gravy boat on the table, spilling a dollop and wiping it up with her forefinger.

"You wear awfully tight pants," Cleo said. "I don't see how you can go to the . . . well, you know, the ladies' room if you're in a hurry."

"Practice."

Hilton sat in gloomy silence. He had felt for some time now that things were getting out of hand, that he had no control over Cleo or Frieda or the servants. Even the gardener's dog, Zia, didn't acknowledge his presence when he walked down the driveway to get the paper in the morning.

Bad manners and taxes and crime and Democrats and unsuitable subjects for dinner conversation were sweeping the country. He was only forty-five and he wanted to stop the world and get off.

"I would rather be exceptional wearing tight pants," Cleo said.

Hilton sighed and served the scrawny rock hens which reminded him of Cleo, and the wild rice which was only grass from Minnesota, and the asparagus which he hated.

"Why couldn't I be exceptional wearing tight pants? Why not?"

"Please don't argue with me, Cleo."

"Why can't I wear . . ."

"Because that style of dress is not suitable for you."

"Why isn't it?"

"There's a stranger in our house. We don't air our personal problems in front of . . ."

"I'm going to tell on you. I'm going to tell everybody."

"They won't listen to you."

"Oh, yes, they will. I have rights."

Hilton ate the scrawny little hen that reminded him of Cleo, and the wild rice which was really grass and the asparagus which he hated. His hands shook.

"I have rights," the girl said again softly.

Later that night Ted came home on his semester break from college. He'd hoped to arrive in time to make a pass at Lisa but she'd already left and he went up to his room alone. He rolled a joint with some pot he'd bought from an assistant professor who'd allegedly smuggled it in from Jakarta. More likely it was grown in somebody's backyard, but he lit up anyway, stripped to his shorts and lay down on the bed.

He was a good-looking young man, tall and heavyset like his father. His long brown hair reached almost to his shoulders in spite of Hilton's attempts to get him to cut it. He wore a beard which his parents hadn't seen yet and were certain to squawk about. But after the first couple of puffs he didn't care.

He was only halfway through the joint when there was a knock on the door.

"Who is it?"

"Me. Let me in."

He opened the door and Cleo came into the room. She was wearing a pink nightgown, not quite transparent.

"Hey, go and put some clothes on," Ted said by way of greeting. "The old boy will have a fit. He thinks I'm a sex maniac."

"Are you?"

"Sure."

"What do sex maniacs do?"

"Oh, Christ, beat it, will you?"

"You're smoking that funny stuff again, aren't you? I could smell it all the way down the hall."

"So?"

"Give me a puff."

"Why?"

"Donny Whitfield says it makes you feel keen. I want to feel keen."

"Well, at least you don't have to worry that it will damage your brain."

She took a puff and immediately let the smoke out again, then sat down on the bed. "I don't feel keen."

"You should inhale and hold it. Like this."

"Okay." She made another attempt. "Your beard looks awful."

"Thanks."

"May I touch it?"

"If you're that hard up for a thrill, go ahead."

She touched his beard, very gently. "Oh. Oh, it's soft. Like a bunny."

"That's me, *Playboy* bunny of the year. Now haul your ass out of here."

"You talk dirty," she said. "Give me another puff."

"I will if you promise to leave right afterwards."

"I promise."

She inhaled the smoke, holding it in her lungs for a few seconds. "I think I'm beginning to feel keen. But I'm not sure—I never felt keen before."

"You promised to leave."

"In a minute. I haven't had a chance to ask you the question I came to ask you."

"Go ahead."

"Do you think I'd look good in tight pants, the kind Lisa wears?"

"How the hell would I know?"

"I could show you my figure."

"Hey, wait a minute. For Christ's sake, don't . . ."

But she'd already taken off the pink nightgown and was standing naked, pale and shivering as though she had a chill. She didn't have a chill.

Ted closed his eyes.

"Ted, are you sleeping?"

"Yeah."

"You didn't even look at me."

"I looked enough."

"Well, what do you think?"

"About what?"

"Gosh, you must have foggy moments like me. You haven't paid any attention. I asked you a question."

He sat up on the bed. Sweat was pouring down the back of his neck.

"Are you having a foggy moment, Ted?"

"Yeah."

"You're not sleeping, are you, Ted?"

"No."

"You haven't even looked at me yet."

"I looked enough."

"I like being here with you, Ted, you know? It's cozy. Do you like it too?"

"Yeah."

She sat down on the bed beside him. Their thighs were touching and he could feel the quiver of her body and her warm breath against his neck.

"Cleo . . . listen. You better . . ."

"Now I've even forgotten the question I was going to ask you and it was terribly important. Oh, now I remember. Do you think I should wear tight pants like Lisa?"

"Not now," he said in a whisper. "Not for a while."

"You're feeling real keen, aren't you, Ted?"

"Lie down."

"What if I don't want to?"

"You want to."

He put one hand between her legs. She let out a squeal and fell back on the bed.

Hilton was awakened by the sound of a car. He thought it must belong to a neighbor, since Ted wasn't due to arrive until the following morning and his arrival was usually accompanied by the blare of a stereo and the whine of tires.

Hilton lay for a long time listening to the night sounds, the ones he hated: Frieda snoring in the adjoining room, the dog Zia barking at a stray cat; and the one he liked: the song of the mockingbird which could begin any time of the day or night. During the day it seemed a medley of all the noises in the neighborhood, coos and rattles and squawks and shrieks, but at night it was mainly a pure clear whistle, the same phrase repeated over and over again, like an impressionist revealing his true self only after the audience had left.

There were other sounds, too: a cricket in the rosebush outside Hilton's room and the rolls and gurgles of hunger inside his stomach. He got up, put on a robe and slippers and went out into the hall intending to go down to the kitchen for some milk and crackers. Before he reached the top of the stairs he saw a light shining under the door of Ted's room at the end of the hall.

Hilton stood listening. Ted's presence was always accompanied by noise of one kind or another, but tonight there was none, not even faint music from a radio. He thought

Frieda or the day maid had left a light on after cleaning the room to have it ready for Ted.

He opened the door. Two people were lying across the bed, their bodies so closely entwined they looked like one, a monster with two heads. It wasn't the first time Ted had sneaked a girl into his room, and Hilton had started to close the door before he realized the girl was Cleo.

A scream formed in his throat, froze, melted, trickled back down into his chest. The two bodies separated and became two.

"God almighty," Ted said and sat up on the bed.

"Get dressed," his father said, "and get out."

"Oh, for Christ's sake, this is some homecoming."

"Put your robe on, Cleo."

"I don't have a robe," Cleo said. "Only that pink nightie Frieda gave me for my birthday."

"Here." Hilton took off his own robe and covered her with it.

"Are you mad at me, Hilton?"

"No."

"Cross your heart and hope to . . ."

"Please be quiet."

"He's mad at me," Ted said. "I'm the villain."

"You are a despicable cad," Hilton said. "And I want you out of this house tonight."

"I've been driving all day. I'm tired."

"Not too tired, I notice. Now move. And don't come back to this house, ever."

"Well, for Christ's sake, how do you like that," Ted said. "This crazy kid comes in here naked and flings herself at me and . . ."

"Shut up. Get moving and don't come back to this house. Ever."

"This is crazy, I tell you."

30

"Cleo, go to your room. I want to talk to you."

"You are mad at me. I," the girl said, "I knew it, I just knew it. And I didn't come in here naked. I had my nightie on and I took it off to show Ted what my figure looked like, in order to get his opinion."

"It seems to have been favorable." Hilton walked out into the hall and after a minute the girl followed him, dragging the pink nightgown on the floor behind her like a guilty conscience.

In the blue and white room whose furnishings had not been altered since she was a child, Cleo sat in a white wicker rocking chair that creaked and squawked with every move she made. Hilton stood with his back to her, facing the wallpaper Cleo had been allowed to choose for herself: masses of white flowers and green leaves and blue-eyed kittens.

"Stop that," he said. "Stop that rocking."

"You are mad at me."

"I'm disappointed."

"It's the same thing."

"No."

"Is Ted going away?"

"Yes."

"Forever and ever?"

"He won't be living in this house anymore." His voice shook. "Are you sorry for what you did?"

"I guess. If you want me to be."

"I want you to be sorry."

"Okay, I am."

He knew he might as well be talking to one of the blue-eyed kittens romping across the wallpaper, but he couldn't stop trying. "I love you. You realize that, don't you, Cleo?"

"Oh, sure. You're always telling me."

"Do you love me in return?"

"Sure."

"No, you don't," he said in a harsh whisper. "You care about nothing."

"Oh, I do so. I love Zia and ice-cream cones and TV and flowers and strawberries. . . ."

"And where do I rate on that scale—somewhere between ice-cream cones and strawberries?"

She'd begun to rock again, very fast, as if to outdistance his voice, and muffle the funny little sounds that were coming from her mouth. These were the sounds of her foggy moments. After a time they would go away.

"Cleo, answer me. Where do I fit on that scale of yours?"

"I have to love Zia best," she said slowly, "because he never gets mad and when I talk to him he always listens like I was a real person."

He turned and grabbed the back of the wicker chair to keep it quiet. "You *are* a real person, Cleo."

"Not like the others. You said I didn't care about things. Real people care about things."

"I didn't mean that. I'm sorry. I'm terribly sorry."

"That's all right."

"Cleo." He fell on his knees beside her, and began stroking her hair. "Promise me something. You must never let another man touch you. Will you promise me that?"

"Sure," she said. He smelled nice, nicer than Ted.

In the morning Ted's BMW was missing and the only sign he'd come and gone was a pair of skis taken from the roof rack and thrown alongside the driveway.

The ski season was over.

From the breakfast room the sounds of quarreling began as soon as it was light outside. Loud sounds, soft sounds, then loud again, depending on who was talking, Frieda or Hilton.

Cleo stared up at the ceiling and listened. Frieda was such a good screamer that every word was clear: Ted was her son as well as Hilton's. . . . Hilton had no right to kick him out so cruelly, his very own son. . . . It wasn't even Ted's fault, it was hers, that damned girl, spoiled, spoiled rotten. . . . She didn't know right from wrong and had no intention of learning. . . . It was Hilton who spoiled her, letting her twist him around her little finger, setting him against his own son. . . . And what if she had a baby? . . . All these damned morons should be sterilized. . . .

Cleo put her hands over her ears but the sounds sifted in through the open window, seeped up through the floorboards and under the cracks of doors like poison gas . . . your fault . . . sacrificed the whole family . . . damn morons should be sterilized . . . spoiled brat . . . one bad apple spoils the whole barrel. . . .

She rolled her head back and forth on the pillow, smothering the words in feathers. She wasn't an apple, a brat, a moron. She was Cleo.

"I am Cleo," she said aloud. "I got rights."

2

WOMAN

3

During the next few days Aragon thought of the girl off and on in a desultory way. It wasn't until Thursday that he had reason to remember her more vividly. A card was brought into his office by the receptionist: Hilton W. Jasper. The card made him think of the girl's high, thin voice repeating, "Hilton says . . . Hilton says."

He told the receptionist, "Send him in here."

"Here?"

"It's the only place I have."

"It's a mess. This man looks important, you know, like in m-o-n-e-y."

"Send him in anyway. He might enjoy slumming."

Hilton Jasper wasn't quite what Aragon expected. A tall, well-built man in his forties, he was almost handsome except for the puffiness around his eyes and the thin, tight mouth.

"Mr. Aragon?"

"Please sit down, Mr. Jasper."

"Thank you." He sat in the same straight-backed cane chair his sister had occupied. "We haven't met, Mr. Aragon. I didn't even know of your existence until an hour ago. Now it seems you may be very important to me."

"In what way?"

"I have a young sister, Cleo. Her welfare is of prime concern to me." He paused. "I have reason to believe she came here the day before she disappeared."

"She came to my office on Monday afternoon."

"Why? Oh, I'm aware of the confidentiality between lawyers and clients but I can hardly consider my sister a client. She had no reason to seek legal advice. Everything has always been taken care of for her. The idea of her coming to a law office is quite incomprehensible to me. Unless—and I'm forced to consider this possibility—she was interested in you personally."

"No."

"You're young, I thought there was a possibility . . . She's so innocent. She has this habit of taking a fancy to people, of trusting them."

"I saw her Monday the first and last time. Her visit lasted fifteen minutes approximately. And that's just what it was, a visit. She didn't seem to be in any kind of trouble that would require the services of an attorney."

"Thank God for that."

"Would you like a glass of water, Mr. Jasper?"

"No."

Aragon poured one anyway from the pitcher on his desk into a paper cup. Jasper drank it.

"Did she appear normal to you, Mr. Aragon?"

"Normal is a pretty big word."

"Not big enough to include Cleo, I'm afraid."

"While she was here she behaved in a responsible manner. I don't give I.Q. tests."

"What brought her here?"

"What brought you, Mr. Jasper?"

"A private detective I hired traced her movements on

the day before she disappeared. He found out she took a taxi from the school during the lunch hour. She told my wife and me that she'd spent the afternoon at the museum. I didn't believe it. The museum's closed on Mondays. Anyway, the taxi driver said he drove her to this office. So here I am. . . . The school knows nothing, or so they claim. These places never know anything except about collecting money. In that field they're experts."

"You've been to the police?"

"Yes. They were polite, no more."

"They don't get very excited about missing persons because they usually turn up safe and sound. Do you think she ran away, Mr. Jasper?"

"I've had no ransom demands," Jasper said grimly. "Also, she withdrew her entire savings account from the bank, a matter of a thousand dollars. The money won't do her any good, may even make things worse. She's so vulnerable, at the mercy of anyone, anything." He wiped his forehead with the back of his hand. "It never occurred to me she'd draw the money out. I gave her everything she needed, everything she wanted. The account was in her name because I was trying to encourage her to be responsible about money, to save. And she did save, money she got for birthdays, Christmas, things like that."

"Then it was her own money?"

"Yes."

"She committed no crime to get it?"

"No."

"And she's over twenty-one?"

"Yes."

"Are you her legal guardian?"

"Yes."

"You signed a document to that effect?"

"Yes."

"Have you checked it recently?"

"No. It's in one of my safe-deposit boxes. I'm not even sure which one."

"Legal guardianships usually terminate at twenty-one."

"But she's not . . . not competent."

"A judge would have to decide that."

"It's common knowledge."

"Common knowledge is not a term recognized by the courts," Aragon said. He felt uncomfortable with the man, more uncomfortable than he had with Cleo. "I'm not sure what you want from me, Mr. Jasper."

"Help. I must get Cleo back to the safety and security of her own home. But first I have to find her. Where could she have gone, where in God's name could she have gone? We have relatives here and there throughout the country but none of them would take her in. They wouldn't want to be held responsible for her. They know what she is." His voice rose. "No, she's out there alone someplace, probably telling everyone she meets how much money she's carrying, inviting disaster, asking for it. You don't understand how easily a girl like that can be taken in, a mere smile or a kind word. I have to find her."

"You told me you hired a detective."

"Yes, when it became clear the police weren't interested. The detective traced Cleo as far as your office, then he had to fly to Houston to testify in a custody case. It was a poor start. I anticipated a poorer finish and fired him."

"And came here."

"I had you checked out by one of my secretaries. You've looked for missing people before. And you have an additional advantage. You've seen my sister, talked to her, noticed the extent of her incapacity. You know her."

"You don't get to know someone in fifteen minutes."

"Perhaps she told you things."

Aragon thought of all the times he'd heard "Hilton says, Hilton says." "A great deal of her conversation consisted of quotes from you, Mr. Jasper. Your opinions seemed very important to her."

"I thought they were, until last week." A film of moisture appeared in the man's eyes. "I need your help, Aragon. I can pay any amount you ask for."

"It's not up to me. I work for a law firm, and I do what the head of that firm, Mr. Smedler, tells me to do."

"Smedler can be handled." There was a note of contempt in his voice, as though handling people like Smedler was simply routine. "Are you interested in the assignment?"

"Yes. As long as you realize that the girl cannot be forced to return."

"Even if she's mentally and emotionally unstable?"

"I doubt you could prove that. The laws protecting the rights of individuals have become very strict."

"I have never forced her to do anything," he said, but he looked oddly disturbed, as though something he thought hidden had been discovered. "Force is not part of my nature. When you find her you will simply persuade her to come home, where she is loved and safe."

"What caused her to leave. Mr. Jasper?"

"I don't know."

"There were no quarrels?"

"No."

"Even a small disagreement might provoke—"

"I told you, no."

"May I talk to your wife?"

"I think not. She's easily upset. It would be preferable if you dealt entirely with me."

"Cleo mentioned your son, Ted. He might have some information not available to you, Mr. Jasper."

"That's impossible. He's away at college."

"What college?"

"It would be a waste of time to question Ted. Anyway,

why she left isn't the issue. It's where she went that must concern you."

"The two are usually connected."

"Find her," Jasper said. "Just find her."

He made it sound more like an order than a plea.

"Has she ever run away before?"

"No."

"Talked about it?"

"No."

"When was the last time you saw her?"

"Monday night. Cleo and my wife and I had dinner together. During the course of it I asked her how she'd spent her afternoon and she said she had gone to the museum. I was pretty sure the museum was closed on Mondays but she spoke of seeing lots and lots of pictures. I didn't argue. After dinner she went to her room to watch TV. Frieda and I retired early. It's a large house with thick, solid walls that muffle sounds. Perhaps Cleo stayed up late watching TV. At any rate, she didn't appear for breakfast and we didn't waken her. I left for the office and Frieda went to a meeting. We assumed that when the school bus came to pick her up she would board it as usual. The cook says she saw the bus waiting in the driveway when she arrived for work but didn't see Cleo get on it. . . . That's all."

It didn't sound like all, or even like half. Jasper seemed to realize this too.

"I can't tell you everything," he said, "because I don't know everything. I've acted *in loco parentis* for fourteen years, ever since Cleo was eight, and I thought I understood the girl. It appears now I was wrong. The lie about how she'd spent the afternoon may not have been the first, perhaps only one of a hundred. I say perhaps. Again I don't know."

The admission was obviously difficult for Jasper.

Though the room was chilly, he wiped his forehead as if being wrong or even doubtful gave him a fever.

"The school called Tuesday afternoon to see if Cleo had stayed home because of illness. They keep close watch on these matters because many of the students are highly susceptible to contagious diseases. So that's how we discovered she had gone."

"Did she take anything with her?"

"Yes."

"Clothes? Suitcase?"

"The dog," Jasper said. "She took the dog, Zia."

He pressed a handkerchief against his mouth and the noise it stifled could have been a cough, a laugh, a cry of rage.

"The dog," he repeated. "It's a basset hound belonging to our gardener, Trocadero. The old man's heartbroken. He saw her leave the grounds with the dog at midmorning and thought she was going to take a run on the beach, which is only three blocks away. He spent the afternoon searching for the dog, calling the Humane Society, the Animal Shelter, even the police. After the school called in the late afternoon I did some searching myself, but not for the dog. I drove around to various neighbors, called friends, checked the bus station, the airport, even the two local car rentals, though I knew Cleo couldn't drive. Finally I went to Troc's apartment over the garage and told him Cleo had run away and taken Zia with her. He didn't believe me."

"What did he believe?"

"That someone had picked them up in a car. He had no proof, nothing to go on but a hunch. He claims Zia weighs sixty-five pounds, much too heavy for Cleo to lift, let alone smuggle aboard a bus or plane. Troc placed an ad in the lost-and-found column of the local paper offering a fifty-dollar reward for the return of the dog, no questions asked.

The ad appeared in this morning's paper. So far there have been no answers."

He paused, staring out the window with its view of the city. Every day it seemed to be crawling farther up the mountain that separated it from the desert beyond. It was a small city but it looked suddenly enormous, capable of hiding hundreds of lost dogs and young girls.

Jasper turned back to face Aragon. "Do you recall the three girl hitchhikers who were murdered here last year?"

"Yes."

"So do I." The bodies of two of the girls had been found at the bottom of a wooded canyon, partially decomposed. The third body was picked up by a fishing boat beyond the kelp line, bloated by decomposing gases and mangled by sharks.

"Don't borrow trouble," Aragon said. "The interest is too high."

"Have you any more concrete advice?"

"You might follow up on that ad. Increase its size, change the wording from *return of the dog* to *leading to the return*. And increase the reward to five hundred dollars."

"I can pay more. Any amount."

"Try it this way first."

"I considered inserting an ad for Cleo herself, with a picture and description and so on, but Frieda vetoed the idea. She has too much of what she terms pride. I'm not sure that's the right word. At any rate I didn't go against her wishes. Things are bad enough without that."

"There's a hot line for runaways that pretty well covers the country. If she changes her mind and wants to come home, you'll hear about it."

"She wouldn't know about such a thing as a hot line. She's very unworldly."

"You said she watches TV."

"Yes."

"A lot?"

"Yes."

"Maybe she's not as unworldly as you think, Mr. Jasper."

Jasper stirred in his chair like a boxer evading a punch. "I'd better be leaving. I'm already late for an appointment. ... Are you going to help me find her, Aragon?"

"I have to wait for orders."

"They'll come."

When he went out to the parking lot at five-thirty he found Charity Nelson waiting beside his old Chevvy. For purposes of shade the space with his name on it was the best in the lot, but the shade was provided by a eucalyptus tree and the owners of newer vehicles took pains to avoid it. The Chevvy stood in splendid isolation, its already pockmarked finish immune to the tree's oily drippings.

Charity was leaning against the hood, fanning herself with an envelope.

"When are you going to get rid of this old heap, Aragon?"

"When somebody gives me a new heap."

"Maybe this is a down payment." She patted her handbag. "Want to guess what's in here?"

"A love letter."

"Close. Love and money are like ham and eggs in Smedler's mind. ... Here. Better cash it, junior, before the old boy discovers he's flipped."

Aragon opened the envelope she gave him. It contained a check for two weeks' salary and a note in Smedler's handwriting: *Giving you 2 wks leove of obsence. Don't blob. WHS.*

"Blob?" Aragon said. "Is this in code?"

"Smedler makes his o's and a's alike. He's giving you two weeks' leave of absence and doesn't want you to blab to the others in the office. . . . Why did you ask him for a leave of absence?"

"I've contracted an obscure tropical disease which requires prolonged—"

"Come off it. Why did you ask him?"

"I didn't."

"Then he really has flipped. Kind of a shame. He's not actually a bad guy underneath all that evil."

He got in the car and turned on the ignition but Charity didn't take the hint.

"I bet I know just where you're heading, junior," she said. "To San Francisco to see your wife."

"Mr. Smedler orders me not to blob, I don't blob."

"He didn't mean me. He couldn't. I'm his confidential secretary."

"You are a blobbermouth and he knows it."

"Oh come on, junior. Just give me a hint."

"I'm going back to school," Aragon said with some truth. "I need a refresher course."

4

Holbrook Hall was located on the former estate of a turn-of-the-century cattle baron. Its stone walls were part of a government work project of the thirties but the main gate with its electronic eye was strictly modern and so were the outbuildings scattered here and there throughout the grounds. They were redwood structures that looked like bungalows.

The atmosphere was strangely quiet for a school. There was no shouting, no laughter, only the noise of a power mower and the whinnying of horses. As he passed the corral Aragon saw that two of the horses were under saddle and had recently been ridden too hard and too fast. A moment later the riders came into view, a pair of adolescent boys wearing western boots and cowboy hats pulled down over their foreheads. At the sound of the car they raised their thumbs for a ride.

Aragon opened the door and they both got in the front. They were about fourteen years old, dirty, tired and morose. Tears mingled with sweat, and water leaked from the canteens they carried.

"What are you guys up to?"

"Nothing."

"Not a thing."

"We took a ride."

"We got caught."

"We going visit my mom in New York."

"We forgot the sandwiches."

"We going to surprise her."

"My mom too."

"She's not your mom. We're not brothers."

"My mom's right tight close by in New Orleans."

"We forgot the sandwiches."

The boys were let out at one of the bungalows and Aragon proceeded on up the driveway to the main house of the estate, a Mediterranean-style classic. Its tile-floored foyer served as the school's reception room.

At one of the desks a young man sat typing, slowly and thoughtfully, as though he was writing his memoirs. The other desk was empty except for a large blue bird eating peanuts. The nuts were being shelled for him by a teenaged girl with the slant-eyed, sweet-tempered look of a Down's syndrome child.

The man said, "Knock it off, Sandy. We have company."

"A friend?"

"Sure."

The girl rose, the bird flew out the window, and the young man turned back to Aragon.

"Are you Mr. Aragon?"

"Yes."

"Mrs. Holbrook's expecting you. Lovely morning. Nothing beats spring. Come this way."

Mrs. Holbrook's office with its red leather upholstery and semicircular desk was more imposing than its occupant. She was a tiny woman with short curly white hair and dimples and soft blue eyes that appeared somewhat baffled.

"Please sit down, Mr. Aragon."

"Thanks."

"This is a distressing situation. A school like ours is hard hit by any scandal. We are dependent on grants and donations. Our fees are high but they simply don't cover our costs and we need benefactors like Mr. Jasper. He's been very generous in the past. . . . And there's Cleo herself, of course. She must be considered."

"Yes." He wondered how far down on the consideration list Cleo rated.

"The other students don't know, naturally. I let it out that she was suffering from chicken pox—I picked something contagious just in case any of them thought of going to visit her. . . . I must say I'm surprised at Cleo. It's not like her to do something like this."

"What is like her?"

"To withdraw when things don't suit her, to refuse

food and wander by herself down to the stable or the poultry pens. These young people often have a strong rapport with animals. She's a timid girl, overindulged, overprotected. A positive step like running away and being able to stay away this long is quite amazing. Nothing has prepared me for it. Well, practically nothing."

"Does 'practically nothing' mean a little something?"

She hesitated before replying. "At the last staff meeting Cleo's name came up. One of the counselors reported that she seemed to be gaining self-confidence, was even getting a little feisty. He felt it was a step forward and the others agreed."

"By others, are you referring to teachers or counselors?"

"Here they're the same thing. We avoid the word *teacher* because it sometimes has a negative connotation these days."

"What counselor made the observation about Cleo at the staff meeting?"

"Roger Lennard."

"Did he have a special interest in Cleo?"

"Not in the way you might mean," she said dryly. "We hire as counselors for the girls men who are not—ah, interested in women. And vice versa for the boys. It minimizes staff-student romances, which can be a problem even in a place like this. Some of the parents refuse to admit that these young people have the same sexual drives as other young people. We deal with them as best we can."

"There's no chance that Cleo was romantically involved with Mr. Lennard?"

"None?"

"None."

"He's gay as a goose."

She walked to the other end of the room, pausing to straighten one of the class pictures hanging on the wall.

She had a small, neat figure and her yellow linen suit looked expensive. She wore no jewelry except a wedding band.

"Exactly what's the matter with Cleo, Mrs. Holbrook?"

"Most likely a combination of things. It's hard to separate mental retardation from emotional retardation. Cleo's a dependent, passive little creature. She's never made a decision in her life, never been expected to, wouldn't be allowed to, probably. So we can't tell for sure how she'd act on her own. I myself suspect that among other factors she has a mild form of epilepsy. But our attempts to get an electroencephalogram were unsuccessful. As soon as she saw the needles she became hysterical and the Jaspers took her home. For accurate results, the patient's cooperation in an EEG is necessary, so no further attempts were made. What a pity. Because if epilepsy should turn out to be part of her problem, it can be treated. Another method of treatment, of course, would be complete separation from her brother and his wife. . . . Here I go again, speaking out of turn, diagnosing, practicing medicine without a license. But when you've been in a place like this for over thirty years you see so much repetition it tends to make you oversimplify. Cleo is, like all of us, complex. As we say, exceptional."

She glanced at the door. It was as definite a dismissal as if she had pointed at it and ordered him to leave.

Aragon said, "Let's review briefly, Mrs. Holbrook. In your opinion, it was unusual for Cleo to take a direct action like running away, and even more unusual for her to stay away this long."

"Yes."

"Yet there is some evidence, according to counselor Roger Lennard, that she was becoming more self-sufficient."

"That's right."

"Are you quite sure that Mr. Lennard and Cleo—"

"Quite, quite sure. Roger was the one who brought her name up at the staff meeting. If there was any relationship between them, he certainly wouldn't have advertised it."

"How do you feel about Cleo, Mrs. Holbrook?"

"I can't afford to get personally involved with any one student. It diminishes my ability to deal with the others." The telephone on her desk rang and she went to answer it. "Yes? . . . Lund and Johnston, that's a first, isn't it? . . . Are the horses all right? . . . Send the boys in. *After* they've showered." She hung up and turned back to Aragon. "I hope Cleo's little caper hasn't started a trend."

"I thought the students hadn't found out about it."

"They found out," she said with a sigh. "Somehow they always do. One way or another, they always do."

Under the oak tree where Aragon had left his car a young man was sitting eating out of a giant bag of corn chips. He was about eighteen, very fat and red-faced, and there was an asthmatic wheeze in his voice when he spoke:

"Hey, man."

"Yes?"

"Want a chip?"

"No, thanks."

"Hear anything from Cleo?"

"Cleo who?"

"Cleo who, that's a hot one. Who you trying to kid? Cleo who. That chicken pox story is a riot. They must think we're a bunch of kooks. Want to hear my opinion?"

"I do, yes."

"She's been kidnapped. The reason the kidnappers haven't asked for ransom yet is they're giving old man Jasper time to get all shook up. The more shook up he gets the more he'll be ready to kick in with a bunch of bucks to get her back. Think about it."

Aragon thought. "Is your name Donny Whitfield?"

"Yeah. How'd you know?"

"Cleo mentioned you."

"Yeah? What'd she say? She kinda likes me, wants to share my space?"

"We didn't discuss that. She talked about the school cruise to Catalina on your father's yacht."

"Oh, that. Big deal. The old boy likes to dress up and play captain." The corn chips were all gone. Donny began on a package of M&M's. "What a clown."

"Were you on that cruise, Donny?"

"Sure. Me and the first mate, we used to do business together."

"What kind of business?"

"What makes you think I'd tell you? You're probably a narc."

"No."

"I'm not telling anyway. It might spoil future deals."

"Where did you go on that Easter cruise, Donny?"

"Just Catalina. Dragon Lady Holbrook didn't trust us any further. In fact, she wouldn't have trusted us that far except my old man told her we couldn't get into any trouble because there was no trouble to get into. Not that Cleo would anyway. She's more goody-goody than the rest of us. Most of us aren't. What a square. She's afraid to breathe unless her old man tells her to. Pitiful."

"He's not her old man, Donny. He's her brother."

"Same diff. He's the boss, he calls the shots."

The boy coughed, aiming some chocolate spit at the oak tree. It dribbled down the bark like tobacco juice. "You headed for town?" he said, wiping his mouth with his forearm.

"Yes."

"I know where they sell some pretty good grass. You buying?"

"No."

"Aw come on, man. Let's go. I can ride in the trunk as far as the gate, then I'll sit up front with you."

"I don't think so," Aragon said. "The trunk's locked and I lost the key."

"Man oh man, that's another chicken pox story. What do you think I am, some nut like the rest of them? You just don't want to give me a ride, right?"

"Right."

"Screw you." The boy stared morosely into the now-empty bag of M&M's. "I bet if I was kidnapped my old man wouldn't pay a dime to get me back."

"I bet he would."

"Naw. He keeps me shut up in this dump so I won't interfere with his chicks. Got any gum?"

"Sorry, no."

"Screw you."

5

Aragon spent the rest of the day at the public library and in the microfilm department of the local newspaper. Hilton Wilmington Jasper was listed as an oil executive and a bank director, born in Los Angeles to Elliot and Lavinia Jasper, a graduate of Cal Tech in Pasadena, married to Frieda Grant, one son, Edward.

The same reference volume listed Peter Norman Whitfield, philanthropist, graduate of Princeton, married five times, one son, Donald Norman Whitfield, and a daughter, deceased.

Ted Jasper was found among the seniors of an old Santa Felicia high school yearbook. The picture showed a smiling blond youth whose sports were listed as tennis and soccer, hobby as girls, and ambition, to attend Cal Poly and become a veterinarian. A current Cal Poly student directory gave his address as 207 Almond Street. When Aragon called the number listed he was told Ted had gone home on the semester break.

An educational journal rated Holbrook Hall as a superior facility for exceptional students. Both boarding and day arrangements. Fees high. Well endowed, established 1951.

No information was available on Roger Lennard.

After a TV dinner and a bottle of beer Aragon phoned his wife. She was a doctor specializing in pediatrics and completing her residency requirements at a hospital in San Francisco. It wasn't an ideal arrangement for a marriage, but it was working and it wouldn't last forever. They planned on living together in Santa Felicia within a year.

Laurie sounded tired but cheerful. "I'm so glad you called, Tom. I get sick of kids. I want to talk to a nice sensible adult."

"What's this, my dedicated wife sick of kids?"

"I'm entitled to a moment of undedication now and then. How about you?"

"Smedler is working in mysterious ways again. I'm expected to track down a runaway retarded girl who maybe isn't so retarded and maybe didn't run away. I have a hunch she might have been coaxed, possibly promised something. She's not a girl, either. She's twenty-two."

"That's a bit old for a runaway."

"She doesn't look her age."

"You know her?"

"I met her once."

"Pretty?"

"Very."

"That complicates matters."

"I'm afraid so."

"A lot of runaways are picked up while trying to hitch-hike. We get quite a few in here. They don't always come out. How are her parents taking it?"

"Coolly. They're both dead. She was raised by a brother at least twenty years older. He's the one who commissioned me to look for her."

"Commissioned? That sounds lucrative."

"Two weeks' pay in advance. More later, perhaps. Very perhaps."

"You don't have a contract?"

"No."

"Really, Tom, who's the lawyer in this family? You should have a contract."

"I don't think Mr. Jasper expects much from me. And he's not the type to pay for what he doesn't get. No little sister, no big bucks."

"How come you bought a deal like that?"

"I didn't buy it. I was sold. . . . Laurie, why do we have to spend all our time talking about other people when we have so much to say about just the two of us?"

"You started it."

"I had all these great things I was going to say to you—"

"Well, it's too late now. Someone wants me in the operating room."

"*I* want you in the operating room," Aragon said. "Or any other room."

"I love you too. Bye."

"Laurie—"

But she'd hung up, and he swallowed all the great things

he had to say to her with the aid of another bottle of beer. Then he called Charity Nelson at her apartment on the West Side. When she answered the phone there were loud staccato noises in the background.

"Hello. I'm too busy to talk. Call back."

"What's all the hubbub?"

"I'm watching an educational program."

"It sounds more like a shoot-em-up western."

"All right." She turned down the sound. "What do you want?"

"Is there any connection between Smedler and Mr. Jasper?"

"How would I know?"

"I have a notion you might have looked it up."

"Of course I looked it up. They're not friends really but they both belong to the Forum Club and serve on a couple of the same boards of directors, the Music Academy and Holbrook Hall. And they have this bond between them that rich men develop—you put your money in my bank and I'll buy stock in your copper mine. It's a great system if you own a bank or a copper mine. The best way to get rich is to start rich."

"Don't let it depress you," Aragon said. "Go back to your shoot-em-up."

"If I had a million dollars—"

"You'd blow it."

"By God, I believe you're right," she said thoughtfully. "But what a blow, junior, what a blow."

"Am I invited?"

"I'll consider it. First, I'd buy me a racehorse. Not one of your ordinary nags but a real thoroughbred with class and guts and stamina. Boy, he'd leap out of that starting gate like a bullet."

"There goes your million."

"You're a wet blanket, junior, a killjoy, a—"

56

"Okay, okay, with my million I'll buy a house in the country where you can keep the horse between races."

"Do you know anything about feeding horses?"

"I thought they fed themselves."

"You're not taking me seriously, junior. Go to bed and have a nightmare."

He went to bed. If he had a nightmare he couldn't remember it when he woke the next morning to the ringing of the phone. A woman identifying herself as Frieda Jasper spoke in a sharp, brittle voice. Making no apology for the earliness of the hour and giving no reason, she asked him to come immediately to 1200 Via Vista.

6

The house, built on a hill overlooking the Pacific, was a two-story adobe with a red tile roof and iron grilling across the lower-floor windows. It looked as though it had been there for a hundred years through a succession of earthquakes, fires and floods. It was a California house, with ice plant covering the ground instead of grass, and landscaped with drought-resistant native plants like ceanothus and sugar-bush.

The woman who crossed the patio to meet him was tall and sturdily built, with a mass of curly red hair just beginning to turn gray. She held a newspaper in one hand, clutching it as though she intended using it to swat a fly or discipline a dog. There were no flies or dogs in sight.

"Mr. Aragon? Please sit down. I thought we'd talk out here on the patio. It's such a pleasant morning."

It was lightly foggy and the wind blowing in from the sea was cold. He buttoned his coat.

"Unless, of course, you would prefer to go inside?"

"Oh, no." The way she was holding the newspaper made him think she would have used it on him if he'd disagreed.

They sat on cushioned redwood chairs with a small redwood table between them.

"My husband was called to Sacramento by the governor for an emergency meeting on offshore oil leases. Only such an important matter would have taken him away from the house at a time like this. He left me with instructions on what to do if anything new developed. The first was to call you immediately. He's taken a liking to you. Hilton does things like that—perhaps every good executive has to." One corner of her mouth curled up in a small, unamused smile. "I know what every executive's wife has to do, and that is obey orders. So here we are, you and I." She made it sound like the opposite of a fun date.

"Has anything new happened, Mrs. Jasper?"

"I think it's going to. Have you seen the morning paper?"

"Not yet."

"It contains the advertisement about the dog. I didn't even have a chance to check it out before the phone began to ring. A man who said he was on welfare described a dog he'd found on his front porch. It was obviously a beagle, not a basset, and I advised him to ask the Animal Shelter to pick it up. The second call was more interesting. A woman with an accent, perhaps Irish, told me that one of her tenants had brought home a dog. She manages an apartment house where dogs are not allowed and she's bringing the dog here in about an hour. It's undoubtedly Zia. She spoke of a small shaved area on the dog's chest where he'd been treated for a hot spot. I'd like you to stay and meet her, Mr. Aragon."

"Did she give a name?"

"Griswold. Mrs. Griswold."

"And address?"

"I forgot to ask. I was terribly rattled. I even had the wild idea that it might be Cleo herself playing a trick on us. She likes to play tricks, but of course anything that elaborate is way beyond her ability."

"Did Mrs. Griswold seem eager to collect the reward?"

"She never mentioned it."

"Not a word?"

"No. I'm prepared to hand it over to her, of course. Hilton left me five one-hundred-dollar bills in case something like this happened. I don't think he expected it though." She glanced at her wristwatch. It was large and serviceable-looking, like Frieda Jasper herself. "We have at least forty-five minutes to wait, assuming Mrs. Griswold arrives on time. I have some coffee made. Would you like some?"

"I would, yes."

The fog was lifting. Steam rose from the swimming pool and the heavy shake roof of the house next door. The sea shone like a bright new revelation. In the distance Mexican palm trees, skinny and shaggy-topped, stood like a row of upside-down dust mops.

She returned carrying a tray with a glass pot of coffee and two ceramic mugs.

"Cream? Sugar?"

"Black."

"Troc's working in the citrus grove out back. I haven't told him yet about the dog. He's old and very emotional and I would be afraid of the consequences if the woman doesn't show up." She sat down again. "We have well over half an hour to wait. I suppose you'll want to ask questions about Cleo."

"Yes."

"The second of the instructions Hilton left me was to be

discreet. I'm not sure I can talk about Cleo and be discreet at the same time. I'll try."

She didn't try very hard. After a swallow of coffee and a couple of deep breaths of air she was off:

"I didn't want to take the girl in. She was eight, a year older than my son, Ted, already fixed in her ways and spoiled by a half-crazy grandmother. But there was no one else willing and able to do it, so she came here. At first Hilton couldn't stand the sight of her because he'd always blamed her for his mother's death. When he came to realize her innocence and her vulnerability, he felt terribly guilty, to blame a child for being born. He gave her everything, everything he had, and unfortunately everything *I* had too. Ted was sent away to school so I could spend more time educating her."

"What did she learn?"

"She learned," Mrs. Jasper said grimly, "whatever she damned well wanted to. Reading? She read quite well indeed if it involved the captions on the pictures in a movie magazine and not a newspaper or book. A selective learner, the educators might call her now. No matter how little she accomplished, Hilton praised her, or rather overpraised her. I went along with it. He was on a guilt trip, you see, and I was his passenger. A fourteen-year guilt trip. God knows how many times I felt we'd come to the end of the line. Maybe this is it."

She finished her coffee and looked into the empty cup as if she hoped to find in it tea leaves that would foretell the end of the line. There was only a coffee stain and a thirsty buffalo fly on the cup's rim.

"I never knew Hilton's mother. Hilton and I didn't meet until after she died. In my high moments I like to think he swept me off my feet and we got married and had a child. My low moments are more realistic. He was grief-stricken and lonely and I was available, the motherly type five years his senior. If there was any sweeping off of feet, I did it. He was smart, handsome and destined for big things."

There was no mention of love, either on his part or hers, either for each other or for the girl. There was only duty, guilt, sacrifice, anger.

"If Hilton's business associates were told some of the things I've told you, Mr. Aragon, they wouldn't believe them. Hilton has a reputation as a cool, unsentimental, hardheaded, hard-driving executive. Our close friends know about Cleo, of course, but we don't have many. I've never had the time for them. Up until this past year, when Hilton agreed to send Cleo to Holbrook Hall, I've been a full-scale babysitter."

"What did Cleo take with her when she left here, Mrs. Jasper?"

"As far as I can tell, nothing. She wore the clothes she usually wore to school."

"In addition to the thousand dollars she withdrew from the bank, did she carry a charge card?"

"Yes, at Drawford's department store."

"Was she accustomed to using it?"

"For Christmas gifts, birthdays, occasions like that. Usually when she shopped I went with her and she used my cards."

She described what Cleo had been wearing on the morning she left with the dog. It was the same kind of outfit Aragon remembered from Cleo's visit to his office, a navy-blue jumper with white blouse and knee socks and black shoes.

"She picked her own clothes," Mrs. Jasper added. "Mostly little-girl stuff. That was partly because she was so small we often had to buy things in the teen department of the store, but it was also her own choice. That is, until recently."

"What happened recently?"

"We hired a new girl to come in and serve dinner every night—Lisa, a college senior. Cleo decided she wanted to dress more like Lisa." She rubbed her left temple with her fingertips as though she were trying to erase a new headache or an old memory. "I guess Hilton's little sister finally decided to become a woman."

From the driveway came the unmistakable noise of an old Volkswagen, followed by the crunch of metal. There were a hundred yards of parking space available, but the VW had chosen to park directly behind Aragon's Chevvy.

A short, stout middle-aged woman wriggled out of the front seat and stooped to examine the two bumpers. Her frown and the way she stood with her hands on her hips indicated that in her opinion Aragon's Chevvy had willfully and deliberately backed into her VW. When she satisfied herself that no damage had been done she opened the front door of the car and a dog jumped out, dragging a length of rope. She attempted to grab the rope but the dog was too fast for her. He made a beeline for the garage, nose to the ground and tail wagging so furiously it was going in a circle. His legs were so short his stomach barely cleared the grass. A loud, full-throated bark announced to the world that Zia was home and in charge.

The woman puffed her way across the patio, trying to explain simultaneously that the dog was a holy terror, wouldn't obey, dragged her every which way, and she hoped it was the right dog because she certainly didn't intend to take it back, not on your life.

Frieda Jasper assured her it was the right dog. "I'm Frieda Jasper, Mrs. Griswold."

"Thank heaven for that. About the dog, I mean. The strength of that mite of a creature you wouldn't believe."

"And this is Mr. Aragon, who is representing my husband in this matter."

Mrs. Griswold, in the act of offering her stubby, sunburned hand to Aragon, suddenly withdrew it. "Representing, what's that mean?"

"I'm one of Mr. Jasper's lawyers."

"A lawyer? Well, if that isn't one for the books, dragging a lawyer into the case of a lost dog. Rich folks sure live different. I wouldn't pay no lawyer for a commonsense thing like a lost dog." Her sharp little eyes focused accusingly on Aragon. "Well, whatever commission you're supposed to get, it's not coming out of my share of the reward."

"I'm on salary, not commission," Aragon said. "You'll receive the reward in full, Mrs. Griswold."

"Oh, no, I won't. I'm only getting fifty dollars for delivering the dog. It's not much, but fair is fair. I didn't find it and I didn't see the ad. It was my tenant, Timothy North. His car's on the blink."

"Can you tell me the circumstances under which he found the dog?"

"He didn't. A man gave it to him. He was in the bar where he works when a man came in and he had this dog with him."

"Can you tell us the name of the bar or its location?"

"No. But it probably was one of those peculiar places, if you catch my gist. Mr. North is a pleasant young man, eats healthy, never touches a drop of booze, but he's—well, peculiar."

"It was a gay bar?"

"I guess that's what they call it."

"Did the man come in alone?"

"My goodness, I wasn't there. They don't like women coming into those places. Anyway, you've got the dog back, so what difference does it make?"

"Perhaps a great deal."

"It said in the ad, 'no questions asked,' and here I am faced with a whole bunch of them. Fraud, that's what it is, fraud, and you a lawyer too. You ought to be ashamed."

"The dog was stolen, Mrs. Griswold, and I'm trying to locate the young woman who stole it."

"My goodness, don't you lawyers have more important things to do than tracking down a dog thief? . . . Now I'll take my money if you don't mind, and be on my way."

"I prefer to hand the money over to Mr. North personally. . . ."

"That sounds like you don't trust me."

"Of course we trust you," Frieda Jasper said. "You volunteered the information that you didn't either find the dog or see the advertisement. Only an honest woman would have done that."

Mrs. Griswold was partly mollified. "Even my worst enemies never called me dishonest."

"However, Mr. Aragon feels he must talk to your tenant because he might have some vital information. Much more is at stake than a stolen dog."

"It's the girl," Mrs. Griswold said. "It's the girl you're after. Well, like I told you before, no girl would have any business going into that bar."

"These places usually have a pretty steady clientele, like an unofficial club," Aragon said. "Perhaps Mr. North knew the man who brought the dog in, or at least could give me a description. Would I find him at home now?"

"He was there when I left. I'm going right back and you can follow me in your car if you want to."

"I'll do that."

Mrs. Griswold's driving proved to be as unorthodox as her parking. She raced through the city streets as though they were roped off for a Grand Prix, and when she hit the freeway she slowed to forty miles an hour and cars honked and passed her on both sides. She finally turned into a driveway without making a signal and Aragon had to slam on his brakes to avoid hitting her.

"You almost hit me," she said when she got out of her VW. "You're certainly not much of a driver. Are you just learning?"

"I've learned quite a lot in the last fifteen minutes."

"I like to set a good example to young people," Mrs. Griswold said virtuously. "I'll be up front in the office if you need me. Mr. North's is number ten, at the far end. You may have to pound pretty hard. He's a bit deaf, being exposed to all that loud music night after night." She turned to go, then suddenly wheeled around to face Aragon again. "What about my reward?"

"Mr. North hired you. I expect he'll pay you."

"He bloody well better or I'll double his rent."

The apartment house was more like a motel, a series of small pink stucco buildings with a carport separating each pair. The inner courtyard contained a live oak tree that looked dead, and a fountain with a bronze dolphin prepared to spout water when someone remembered to turn it on. Number ten was at the rear of the courtyard. Its windows were open and music was playing inside, not the kind of loud rock or disco that Mrs. Griswold had referred to but a soft, melancholy Russian nocturne.

Mr. North's quick response was also unexpected. The door opened before Aragon had a chance to knock.

"Mr. Timothy North?"

"You know it. I saw you out back with Griswold."

The young man's eyes went with the music. They were sad and gray and remote. But he had the body of a weight lifter, overdeveloped chest and biceps that looked ready to burst through his skin as well as his T-shirt. His voice seemed, like his muscles, to have been overused.

He said hoarsely, "The basset was yours, huh?"

"I'm prepared to pay the reward."

"Fine. I'm prepared to accept it." He turned off the music. "I hope it's in cash. What did you say your name was?"

"Tom Aragon."

"And I'm Tim. Tom and Tim. Cute. We could be twins. How about that?"

"If you don't mind, I'd like to ask you a few questions, Mr. North."

"Tim."

"Tim."

"Questions weren't part of the deal, Tom," North said reproachfully. "But you're calling the shots, amigo. You got the dog, you got the money. All I got is egg on my face. Or what might look like egg to somebody suspicious."

"I don't see any egg."

"Okay, come in."

About half of the small room was taken up by an expensive-looking exercise machine. The cologne North had sprayed on himself wasn't quite strong enough to cover the smell of sweat that hung in the air.

North gazed at the machine with parental pride. "Some little contraption, huh? It's a killer. You wouldn't last a minute on it."

"Probably not," Aragon said. "What's the name of the bar where you work, Mr. North?"

"Phileo's. *Phileo,* that's the Greek word for *I love.* Cute, huh?"

"Real cute."

"It's not the kind of place where you'd bring your mother, but we got plenty of action. You ought to drop in sometime."

"Sorry, my mother never lets me go anywhere without her."

"We might make an exception in her case."

"Neither does my wife."

"So you have a wife. You're not wearing a wedding band."

"When we were married we couldn't afford two wedding bands, so we flipped for it. She won. Cute, huh?"

North's shrug indicated that other people's cutes weren't as amusing as his own. Leaning against the exercise machine, he waved his hand in the direction of the couch. "Sit down."

The couch needed cleaning and reupholstering but Aragon sat. "When did you acquire the dog, Mr. North?"

"Night before last. This man comes into Phileo's with a basset hound on a leash. He wasn't one of our regulars. As far as I know I never saw him before. Or since."

There was something bitter in North's voice that puzzled Aragon. "Would you describe him?"

"Medium height, a bit paunchy around the middle. Wavy brown hair thinning on top. I'd guess he was in his middle thirties. Not bad-looking but he had a bad case of the glooms. Nothing like the glooms to kill off a guy's looks. Me, when I feel them coming on I mount Baby here and sweat them away." He patted the machine on what was more or less its rear end. "Anyway, the guy sits down at the table nearest the door and he and the dog are real quiet, minding their own business. As far as I was concerned they could have stayed there. But the boss spotted them right away and sends me right over. I had to tell the guy that dogs weren't allowed in there. He apologized. He said dogs didn't seem to be welcome anyplace anymore, that his landlord had told him to get rid of it or else, and he was looking for someone to take it off his hands. The fact is, I've always been a pushover for dogs and I think he guessed this. I said I'd consider it. I went back to the bar and made some customer a margarita—I distinctly remember it was a margarita—and went back and told the guy okay, I'd take it. It was a real cute dog. I kidded myself that Griswold's little heart would melt at the sight of it. It didn't."

"You said the dog was on a leash?"

"A thin brown leather leash and collar with metal tags."

"It was on a rope when Mrs. Griswold delivered it."

"That was a funny thing. When he gave me the dog he removed its collar with the leash attached, said he wanted something to remember it by. It didn't occur to me until I read the ad in the paper that he didn't want me to see the dog's tags because it was stolen. Was it?"

"Yes, but not by him—by a young woman."

"You can bet the rent it wasn't his woman," North said with a sardonic smile. "Ordinary people don't just drop in Phileo's for a drink. We're out of the way. You have to come looking for us and know what you're looking for. This guy belonged there. He didn't look happy about it. Maybe he was still in the closet or just coming out because he'd discovered closets have glass doors. No matter. He belonged at Phileo's. Taking the dog there with him, that part was unusual. We don't run any far-out joint that involves animals. Besides, he wasn't the type."

"How could you tell?"

"I got X-ray eyes when it comes to people's weaknesses. This guy was depressed, real depressed. I don't say he was sick. He probably had plenty to be depressed about." Once again there was a curiously bitter note in his voice: *so the guy was depressed—serves him right.*

"Would you recognize the man if you saw him again?"

"Bet the rent I would. Faces are my business." North's own face was beginning to show signs of impatience. "Now I think I've answered enough questions for five hundred dollars minus fifty for Griswold. I could slit my throat for offering her fifty. She'd probably have taken twenty. Well, next time I'll know better. Not much chance of that, though, is there?"

"No."

The envelope changed hands. North folded the five crisp new hundred-dollar bills and put them in the back pocket of his jeans. Then he picked up the morning newspaper opened to the want-ad section and kissed it vigorously. "Thank you, *Daily Press*. . . . Maybe I should have it framed. On second thought, maybe I should give it to you for good luck. Here you are, Tom. Good luck."

It didn't turn out that way.

From a public phone booth in the nearest gas station he called the number given in the lost-and-found ad. A woman answered in a heavy Spanish accent:

"This is the Jasper residence. Hello."

"Is Ted there?"

"Just a min— No, no. No, no, no."

There were too many *no*'s. "This is a friend of his from school. I just wanted to say hello."

"He not here. Mr. Jasper not here. Mrs. Jasper not here. Nobody. Nobody home. Ted say nobody home."

"Tell him a friend of his from Cal Poly is passing through town and wants to buy him a drink."

There were sounds of a slight scuffle, a barely audible "Goddam you, Valencia, when are you going to learn?" Then a man's voice:

"Who is this?"

"We were in the same lab last semester."

"I didn't have a lab last semester."

"Maybe I have the wrong Jasper. Theodore?"

"Edward."

"Wrong Jasper, obviously. Sorry. It was a natural mistake."

"Not so natural," Ted said. "We're not listed in the

phone book. . . . Who is this anyway? And what do you want?"

Aragon hung up. It was a stupid error, not checking the telephone directory. But he had the notion that Ted wouldn't have been of much help under any circumstances. He sounded like a very angry and suspicious young man.

7

It was still morning, though it felt later. The hours spent with Frieda Jasper, Mrs. Griswold and Timothy North seemed to have spread across a whole day like an oil spill, leaving black stains and the smell of tar.

He drove to Holbrook Hall for his second visit of the week. Halfway up the long steep driveway, two older students were preparing to have a picnic lunch under an enormous fig tree. A third was in the tree itself—Donny Whitfield, his fat, sunburned legs dangling like meat on a hook. He let out a yell when he saw Aragon's car.

"Hey. Hey, wait up!"

Aragon stopped. The boy dropped out of the tree and came stumbling across the lawn. He got in the car, breathing noisily.

"Jeez, am I glad to see you." Aragon wished he could say the same, but everything about Donny seemed swollen—his short puffy fingers, his cheeks distended like those of a squirrel storing food for winter, his thighs bulging out of the cutoff jeans. Even his eyelids looked blistered from the heat of either tears or sun.

He said, "I forget your name."

"Tom Aragon."

"Listen, man, I got to split this dump. They put me on a diet, me and those two back there. All we're allowed for lunch is lettuces and cottage cheese, rabbit food, yuck. They even locked the candy machine. How's that for a low blow? You don't happen to have a chocolate bar on you?"

"No."

"Pack of Life Savers?"

"No. Sorry."

"Screw you."

"You told me that yesterday."

"So? It still goes. If you help me get out of here, I bet I could help you find Cleo. I know about chicks from all my dad's chicks. They're the same, even a nut like Cleo. How about it, do we have a deal?"

"What happened to the kidnapping theory you had yesterday?"

"Down the drain. I figure now that she flew the coop. A lot of my dad's chicks did the same." Donny removed the huge wad of chewing gum from his mouth, examined it critically and put it back in. "Look, man, I'm ready to deal. I can lay my hands on some money. You must need money or you wouldn't be driving this hunk of rust. How about it?"

"You're not actually a prisoner here, are you, Donny?"

"You want to know what would happen if I walked out without one of those dimwit counselors tagging along? They'd call the cops."

"Why?"

"I'm on probation. If I stick around here, I stay out of the slammer. It was a bum rap. I don't belong with the cra-

zies you see in this joint. I'm not retarded either. I got an
A in school once. Want to guess what in?"

"Tell me."

"Eating," the boy said somberly. "It was a joke, ha ha."

"What bum rap did they pin on you, Donny?"

"That was long ago and far away, man. Anyway, my dad
fixed it. He's a great fixer, dear old dad, specially when it
leaves him free to mess around with the chicks without
competition from me. Maybe you think I'm not much
competition, right?"

"I'm not a chick," Aragon said. "I have to go up and see
Mrs. Holbrook now. Want to come along for the ride?"

"Naw. She makes me puke."

Waiting in the small reception room outside Mrs. Holbrook's office, Aragon wondered what the charge against
the boy had been. Donny wasn't likely to talk, Mrs. Holbrook probably even less so, and juvenile records were
often ordered sealed by the judge in the case.

Mrs. Holbrook greeted him with a neat professional
smile. She did not sit down or ask him to sit down. The
omissions seemed a neat professional way of informing him
that she was busy and suggesting that, even if she weren't,
his presence wouldn't be welcome. It was evident that she
sensed trouble.

She said, "I gather nothing's been heard from Cleo?"

"Nothing."

"I'm afraid I can't be of any further help, Mr. Aragon. I
gave you all the information you asked for yesterday."

"Perhaps not quite all, Mrs. Holbrook. I'd like to speak
to Roger Lennard."

"He hasn't been at work most of this week."

"That was one of the things you didn't tell me yesterday."

"You didn't ask yesterday."

"How long has he been absent from the school?"

"He called in last Wednesday morning and said he had the flu. We have to be extremely cautious, since some of our students are very susceptible to such contagions, so I told him to stay home until he felt better. He did. There's no mystery about Mr. Lennard's absence. I hope you've abandoned that silly idea of any romantic attachment between Mr. Lennard and Cleo."

"I may have other silly ideas," Aragon said. "How long has he worked here?"

"Since last Christmas, when one of our regular counselors left for Europe on a Fulbright scholarship."

"Can you give me Lennard's address and phone number?"

She opened a drawer of one of the maroon-painted filing cabinets that lined the rear wall.

"His address and phone number are still the same as these on his application form. Four hundred Hibiscus Court, Space C, telephone 6823-380. I still don't understand why you insist on dragging Mr. Lennard into this. Roger is a conscientious young man, totally dedicated to his students. He tries to make them feel normal, human, not social outcasts."

"Is there a picture of him in his file, Mrs. Holbrook?"

"Yes."

"May I see it, please?"

The picture was almost as vague in detail as the description Timothy North had provided of the man with the basset. It could have been almost any dark-haired youngish man trying to look earnest on an application form for an earnest-type job.

"Do you mind if I borrow this?"

"It's beginning to look," Mrs. Holbrook said grimly, "as

though you're determined to discredit our school. I've a good notion to call Roger right this minute and let him speak for himself."

"That would suit me fine."

She pressed the numbers on the phone and waited a full minute before hanging up. "He's probably asleep," she said.

"Suppose I check that out."

"Go ahead. You will anyway."

"I have to, Mrs. Holbrook."

Timothy North was still working out on his exercise machine in the small stucco bungalow. The pink sweatband around his head had turned dark with moisture. He wiped his face and hands on a towel before glancing at the picture.

"Sure, that's him all right. Not a happy chappy, is he? Well, maybe he has reasons."

"Bet the rent on it," Aragon said.

Hibiscus Court was a mobile-home park separated from the luxury condos along the beachfront by the railroad track, and from the city proper by the rickety old frame houses and buckling sidewalks of the barrio where Aragon had spent his youth.

Space C was occupied by one of the smaller units. It was well-kept, its handkerchief-size lawn trimmed, the azaleas in ceramic pots carefully shaped. The window frames and the posts of the carport were newly painted in light green. A card on the main door bore the name Roger E. Lennard. The venetian blinds on the windows were closed tight and the carport was empty. Aragon knocked anyway. There was no answer.

After a time he became aware of someone watching from

the rear of the building. He turned and said, "Hello? Hello there."

A man stepped out briskly and started walking toward him. There was nothing furtive or guilty in his manner. He gave the impression that spying on a neighbor was merely part of his life-style. The straw sombrero he wore emphasized his shortness. His face was deeply tanned and creased like a piece of paper that had been scorched by the sun and folded and refolded a hundred times.

"Looking for Mr. Lennard?"

"Yes. I'm Tomas Aragon."

"Spanish?"

"Yes."

"Spanish, Latino, Hispanic, Mexican, Chicano—what do you fellows like to be called, anyway?"

"Fellows is good enough."

"No slur intended and none taken, I hope. After all, I'm used to being called a few things myself." He pushed back his sombrero and revealed a head as brown and hairless as a basketball. "Baldy. Curly. Kojak. Don't bother me a bit being called names like that. The real one's Abercrombie."

They shook hands. Then the old man took out a pouch of tobacco and a package of cigarette papers and began rolling himself a cigarette with the clumsiness of a novice. "Trying to save a bit of money, but I can't seem to get the hang of this. I see it done in old movies all the time, slick as a whistle, but it never works out like that for me. Must be trick photography."

"Are you the manager of this place, Mr. Abercrombie?"

"Not exactly. I get a little something off my space rental if I go around making sure the rules are obeyed. No parties or loud television after ten. No dogs or cats or birds that talk."

"Mr. Lennard had a dog, did he not?"

"Not for long, he didn't. To tell the truth, I was surprised at him trying to break the rules like that. Then I found out he was only keeping it for a friend. Mr. Lennard's the quiet type who don't have many friends, so I told him the dog could stay for a day or two until he found another home for it. He must have found one pretty quick because I never heard the dog after that. I haven't seen Mr. Lennard either. Matter of fact, I don't see much of him anyway. During the day he works at that peculiar-like school and at night he often goes out by himself, to the movies or library—that's what I used to think anyway. Like I said, Mr. Lennard's not the type to have a lot of friends. He just came to town last winter from Utah. His car had Utah plates on it, a red Pinto wagon."

Abercrombie lit the cigarette. Some of the burning tobacco fell down the front of his shirt, adding two or three more holes to the dozen already there.

"I got it too loose this time," he explained. "Sometimes it's so tight I can hardly get a drag out of it. Trick photography, that's how they do it in the movies, trick photography. . . . Anyhow, when I went over to tell Mr. Lennard he had to find another place for the dog he handed me a real surprise. He asked me if it was all right if he got married and his wife moved in with him. How's that for a kicker?"

It was a kicker, all right, Aragon thought. And the kickees included himself, the Jaspers, Mrs. Holbrook and her school, and probably most of all, Cleo. "Did Lennard announce the date of his wedding?"

"Right away. 'The sooner the better'—those were his very words."

"Did he appear happy?"

"Excited, more like. And scared too. Marriage is a big step. I never took it myself. Maybe my legs were too short."

Abercrombie paused, obviously expecting a laugh. Aragon obliged. It wasn't very convincing but it seemed to satisfy the old man. He went on:

"I told Mr. Lennard he could bring his bride to live here as long as they didn't have any children. That's another of our rules, no children. Well, sir, you should have seen him blush, just like some pimply little teenager. I said, you'll have to bring the lady around and introduce her to the other people in the court. He said he would but he never did."

"When did this conversation take place?"

"About the middle of the week. I'm not sure what day."

"And where?"

"Right here where we're standing, under the carport."

"You didn't go inside?"

"He never invited me inside. It's not my business to go where I'm not wanted."

"Were the venetian blinds closed, the way they are now?"

"He kept them that way." The old man squinted as he took another puff of the cigarette. "Are you hinting the woman might have been in there all the time I was talking to him?"

"Possibly."

"That's no normal behavior, an engaged man hiding his intended like she had two heads. Unless she's the real shy type. There are a few shy women, I guess. I never get to meet any of them. . . . I didn't think to ask if you were a friend of Mr. Lennard's."

"No."

"You're not a bill collector, are you?"

"Not exactly," Aragon said. But it was time for Roger Lennard to start paying his debts.

* * *

It was midafternoon when he finally stopped for lunch at a taco stand near his apartment. The early morning mist had long since been driven out to sea by a hot dry wind blowing in from the desert on the other side of the mountain. He sat under the thick shade of a laurel tree, sipping iced tea and thinking of Cleo. The evidence was circumstantial but there seemed little doubt that she had run away to marry Roger Lennard. He tried to imagine Cleo as a bride in long white gown and veil or even an ordinary dress, but all he could conjure up was the picture of a skinny, blank-eyed girl wearing a navy-blue jumper and white blouse and knee socks. According to Frieda Jasper, Cleo hadn't taken any clothes with her, so she would probably use the thousand dollars from her bank account to buy a trousseau of some kind. Perhaps, however, she had enough business sense—or Roger Lennard had it for her —to have saved the cash and made any purchases for her wedding at the department store where she held a charge card.

Cleo and Roger. A bride and groom as unreal as the plastic figures on top of a wedding cake, standing on ground no more stable than sugar frosting.

Aragon finished his tea, fed the remaining ice cubes to the laurel tree and the plastic cup to the trash bin and went back to his car. He knew that he had to tell the Jaspers and that the rest of the day would be all uphill. He felt the need to touch home base before going off into another game, so he drove to his office.

Charity Nelson must have been watching the world as she often did from the windows of Smedler's quarters on the top floor. The steel cage of the outside elevator descended the wall and she came charging out, hanging on to her wig so it wouldn't blow off in the wind.

He was glad to see her and told her so.

She looked shocked. "My God, junior, you having a heat stroke or something? Come on up and I'll put a cold pack on your head."

"Where's the boss?"

"Smedler had a very important client who wanted to play golf. Smedler, of course, wanted to stay here and work like a beaver but he forced himself to go to the country club. A man of sacrifice, not so?"

"Not so."

"Come along."

They took the elevator up to Charity's office. It was filled with the plants that were her children, raised from infancy, nurtured, nursed tenderly through diseases: the dieffenbachia whose scale she scraped off with her fingernails, the marantas and crotons she misted night and morning to discourage red spider mites, the coleus whose mealybugs she treated with Q-Tips dipped in alcohol, the Hawaiian elf which required a drink of warm unchlorinated water every noon, the aphelandra which kept losing its limbs to aphids, these were her special darlings. To the hardier plants that could pretty well fend for themselves she gave a good home but little real love.

She perched on the edge of her desk, swinging her legs and examining them critically as they swung. "My legs are the only vestiges of my youth. They're still pretty good, don't you think?"

"Do you want me to tell you you've got great gams?"

"I wouldn't mind."

"You've got great gams."

"Thank you, junior. Now I suppose you want a compliment in return."

"It might be a nice switch."

"Okay. Smedler says you're a young man who's going

places. Of course he didn't specify what places—that's a lawyer for you, can't make a statement without leaving himself an out. . . . Want some orange juice?"

"Please."

She poured the juice not into the small plastic cups beside the water cooler but into the crystal stemware she reserved for special occasions. He wondered what the occasion was and if he had, however reluctantly, played a part in it.

She raised her glass. "Here's to the twenty-third anniversary of my first divorce. His name was Harold and he was a teetotaler. You ever been married to a teetotaler?"

"No."

"It's like being married to an aardvark. It's okay if you're another aardvark. Harold never drank anything but orange juice. It's weird, every time I drink the stuff I think of him. Memories can be a real drag. Anyway, here's to Harold, if he isn't dead of an overdose of vitamin C."

She made a face when she drank the orange juice as if it tasted of Harold.

"Sit down, junior, and tell all."

"Sorry, I have orders from Smedler not to blob, as you may recall."

"I've done a little detective work of my own and found out what you're working on anyway. This man Jasper has big bucks in oil and copper. He's going to be deep-down-in-the-pocket grateful if you find his sister. You could be rich."

"Money can't buy happiness."

"You got that mixed up, junior. Happiness can't buy money, though God knows I keep trying."

"When Mr. Jasper hears what I've got to tell him," Aragon said, "I'll be lucky to get out of this with two cents and a handshake."

"You found her? You actually *found* her?"

"Not exactly. But I know why she went away. It's not the kind of information Mr. Jasper will be happy to hear."

"What happened?"

"She eloped with one of her counselors."

"What's the matter with that? I think it's romantic."

"He's gay."

"Well," Charity said, and again, "Well. That's not quite so romantic, is it?"

"No."

"However, maybe he's only half gay, or three fifths. Or even seven tenths. That would leave—"

"I don't know the exact percentage."

"To a normal woman even a little is too much."

Charity poured another round of orange juice. She was beginning to feel more kindly toward the long-gone Harold. A teetotaler, yes, but he sure as hell wasn't a pansy.

She went on to tell Aragon more about Harold than he wanted to know and certainly more than Harold would have wanted him to know. He listened patiently until, having finished off Harold, she started in on George. George, it seemed, was not a teetotaler. In fact, he drank like a fish.

"But he was not a pansy," Charity said solemnly. "None of my husbands has been a pansy."

"Glad to hear it. Now I have to—"

"George's weakness was blondes. Any size, any age."

"—leave. Goodbye. Keep up the good work."

"What good work? What's the matter with you, junior?"

He stepped into the elevator and the door clanged shut.

"Don't you want to hear about George?"

"Later," Aragon said. Much much later.

When he returned to his car he saw that the lid of the trunk was not completely closed. There were no signs of forced entry and everything was still inside: a box of tools; a nylon jacket belonging to his wife, Laurie; a first aid kit; his beach shoes, the soles encrusted with tar; and an orange that had rolled out of its bag when he'd bought groceries a few nights before. That was the last time he'd had occasion to use the trunk.

He tried unsuccessfully to close the lid. Then he saw what was keeping it partly open. A large wad of chewing gum had been pushed into the lock.

Aragon thought of the desperation on Donny Whitfield's face when they met at Holbrook Hall that morning and it was suddenly clear what had happened. Donny had used the keys, inadvertently left in the ignition, to open the trunk. Then he'd replaced the keys and hidden himself in the trunk. The wad of chewing gum forced into the lock kept the lid from closing tightly and allowed Donny to escape.

Some people would do anything to get off their diets.

8

The plane from Sacramento arrived at twilight. Though Hilton Jasper sat in one of the rear seats he let all the other passengers get off before him. He didn't want to go back to a house without Cleo, without Ted. From the window he could see Frieda waiting for him at the gate, pacing up and down with quick little steps that indicated her impatience. She was always impatient, impatient for night to fall, impatient for morning to begin, impatient to drive him to the airport, to drive him home again. The world moved too slowly for Frieda. She wore herself out trying to hurry it along.

The flight attendant handed him his briefcase. "We're here, Mr. Jasper."

"Yes. Thanks."

"Unless you want to go back to Sacramento with us—"

"I think not."

He stepped out of the plane and Frieda came hurrying to meet him. She took the briefcase out of his hand. It was probably meant to be a loving gesture but there was no love in it. She said, "Everyone got off before you. I thought you might have missed the plane."

"Someone has to be last."

She frowned, as though she was trying to understand this odd bit of philosophy. Frieda was always the first on a plane and the first off. It was as natural to her as any ordinary bodily function.

"You look tired," she said. "Cook made you a lovely dinner. It will take only three or four minutes to heat it up in the microwave."

"I'm not really hungry, Frieda."

"Of course you're hungry," Frieda said in a tone that meant he damned well better be hungry because she was. "And it's especially important that you have a good meal tonight."

"Why?"

"Mr. Aragon is coming over at nine. He has something to tell you. . . . Now please don't get excited, Hilton. The doctor warned you to take it easy. Cleo is all right. She's not dead or injured or any of the dozen things you imagined. I repeat, she's all right. Apparently she just doesn't want to come home."

"Because of Ted—that terrible scene—"

"For God's sake, let's not go into that again. Her decision to leave very likely had nothing to do with Ted. Perhaps she's been planning it for a long time. The girl never confided in me. I never knew what was going on in that head of hers. When I asked her anything personal she'd just stare at me with those funny eyes—"

"Be quiet, Frieda."

They drove home in silence, and they ate in silence in a small alcove off the kitchen which had a view of the mountains. As the sun set each night the mountains gradually turned from violet to midnight blue and finally disappeared. Lights were springing up along the foothills like strings of Christmas decorations.

Frieda served the meal herself. The only live-in maid, Valencia, had gone to her room to watch television, or whatever maids called Valencia did in their rooms. Frieda had never bothered to find out. She felt reasonably sure, however, that the woman, who spoke little English, would not be eavesdropping like the cook or intruding to express an opinion like Lisa, the college girl who served dinner.

"I hate these silences," she said finally. "They're mean, hostile. Can't you think of anything to say?"

"Nothing you'd want to hear."

"All right, I'll say something and you won't want to hear it either. Ted came to pick up his things this morning. I gave him some money. Don't worry, it was from my own bank account."

"Your own bank account came from my own bank account. And I specifically asked you not to give him any money."

"You commanded me not to."

"But you did anyway."

"He's my son. You treated him unfairly, cruelly."

"He did something unforgivable. If it weren't for that,

Cleo would be at home right now, safe and secure."

"And you know where *we'd* be, Hilton? Right here with her for the next ten, twenty, thirty years like the last fourteen, babysitting a girl who's never shown the slightest shred of gratitude, who doesn't even like us."

He dropped his fork on the plate and spit the food from his mouth into a napkin. She knew she had hit him hard and she was almost but not quite sorry that she was going to hit him again.

"If Cleo walked in the front door this very minute," she said," I'd walk out the back. And you and Cleo could live happily ever after."

"What are you implying, you bitch?"

"I'm not implying anything. I'm stating it outright. You and Cleo can live happily ever after as far as I'm concerned. I don't want to be around."

"By God, you are a bitch."

"It took fourteen years of Cleo to make me one."

Outside, the dog Zia had begun to bark, a deep-throated menacing bark incongruous for his size. He paused now and then as if to gauge the effect of his threats, and during these pauses a car engine could be heard.

Hilton got up so fast he almost knocked the table over, and he reached the front door at the same time as Aragon.

"Have you found her?"

"No," Aragon said. "But I'm pretty sure she's all right."

"Thank God for that. Come in. Come in and tell me about it."

They went down the long galleria to the kitchen. Frieda had cleared the dishes off the table and was pouring herself a cup of coffee. She didn't offer any to either of the men.

Aragon sat across the table from Hilton Jasper and began to talk. "For the past few months Cleo has been counseled at school by a man named Roger Lennard. He's in his early thirties and has the reputation of being very conscientious in his work. He evidently gave Cleo some new ideas about herself and indicated some possibilities for her future. At any rate, he and Cleo became involved emotionally. I won't say romantically, because Lennard is a homosexual."

Jasper made a strange choking noise as if he had something stuck in his throat. "And she's with *him?*"

"They're going to be married. Perhaps they already are."

"Cleo doesn't even know what a homosexual is," Jasper said. "She doesn't really know what marriage is."

Frieda spoke for the first time. "She's not the innocent little angel my husband imagines she is. He never let me tell her the facts of life. He said she was too young, too simpleminded. I didn't insist. I assumed they took care of these matters at school. She was certainly no innocent. I know that from"—she gave Hilton a long meaningful stare —"from experience.... Don't we, Hilton?"

"Please don't interrupt, Frieda." And to Aragon: "Tell me more about this Roger Lennard. Where does he live?"

"In a mobile-home court down near the beach. It was one of his neighbors who told me about the impending marriage. Lennard asked permission to have his wife come to live in the unit he rented."

"He must be a real prize, a counselor in a school like Holbrook making a play for one of his students."

"Mrs. Holbrook thinks very highly of him."

"Then she's evidently a poor judge of people."

"Just who made a play for whom?" Frieda said. "That's what I'd like to know."

Jasper went over and put his hand on her shoulder. "You appear tired, Frieda. Perhaps you should go to bed."

"I don't want to go to bed."

"I suggest you reconsider." He pressed his hand down hard on her shoulder. "You want to appear all bright-eyed and bushy-tailed tomorrow at breakfast the way you usually are, don't you?"

"I'm glad she's gone. You hear that, Hilton? I'm glad. She's ruined enough of my life."

"You'd better go to bed."

"Let her ruin somebody else's."

Aragon watched her leave, her heels clicking decisively on the tile floor. It was the first time he'd thought of Cleo as a ruiner, a destructive force, more of a victimizer than a victim.

"Forgive my wife," Jasper said quietly. "This buisness has put a severe strain on both of us. Frieda is just as devoted to the girl as I am."

He didn't sound convinced or convincing and seemed to realize it. He let the subject drop abruptly, as though he'd picked up a rock too hot and heavy to handle.

Aragon rose, ready to leave. "I'm sorry I haven't been able to solve your problem, Mr. Jasper, but this is the end of the line for me."

"Where's Cleo?"

"I made it clear that I don't know."

"Then you haven't done what you were hired to do," Jasper said. "Cleo must be found and rescued."

"By 'rescued' you mean brought back here?"

"Yes."

"The law is pretty specific about kidnapping."

"Use persuasion."

"I'm afraid Roger Lennard has already used persuasion."

"She must be rescued," Jasper repeated. "It's not the homosexual part that worries me most. It's the fact that he's a fortune hunter. Cleo will come into her grandmother's full estate when she's twenty-five. A great deal of money is involved. Cleo is vaguely aware of this, certainly aware enough to have told Roger Lennard about it. But I'm sure she has no idea about the California community property laws or anything involving money. A million dollars in the bank isn't as real to her as a crisp new ten-dollar bill. If someone grabbed the ten-dollar bill from her, she'd resent it and try to get it back or else come crying to me for another one. But a million dollars that she can't see or feel or buy candy with is nothing to her. To Roger Lennard it's everything. He may even be faking a few love scenes. The thought of it makes me sick."

He looked sick. His face had a waxen pallor and there was a fringe of moisture across the top of his forehead. Aragon had acquired a minimal knowledge of medicine from his wife, Laurie, and Jasper appeared to him like a man set up for a heart attack. A big man, an ex-athlete, overweight, with a sedentary job and under a heavy strain, he was programmed for one. Whether it happened or not was a matter of luck, good or bad.

Jasper said, "That bastard Lennard is going to regret this. He'll wish he had stayed in the closet with the door deadlocked!"

"I advise you to wait for the facts before you take any action."

"Then get the facts."

"I'm not trained in police work, or psychology either, for that matter. I don't know where to go from here."

"You got this far. Keep going. If you won't, I will."

"Stay out of it personally, Mr. Jasper, at least until you—"

"Cool down? I don't cool easily."

It wasn't exactly news. The blood had come rushing back into Jasper's face and he looked ready to burst his skin. He slapped his hand flat against the table.

"When I get through with that bastard," he said, "he'll be lucky to get a job as a dishwasher. He's contemptible, a man without moral decency, to take advantage of a girl like Cleo entrusted to his care. God knows what romantic notions he put into her head."

Aragon knew of only one notion, and not by the wildest stretch of the imagination could it be called romantic. He remembered almost precisely the words she'd used on her visit to his office: "My new friend says I got rights, I can do what other people do, like vote." Vote. Lennard's approach was certainly unique.

"I'll do the best I can, Mr. Jasper. But don't expect miracles. Both people involved, Lennard positively, Cleo probably, must be aware that they've asked for trouble."

"I don't expect miracles. I expect results. Go back to where Lennard's been living, examine his personal effects, his correspondence, bank accounts if any, even the books he reads."

"You're asking me to break in."

"No. We won't call it that."

"Others will. Gaining entry to Lennard's place would require a search warrant issued by a judge to a policeman under circumstances strongly suggesting a crime. I don't meet any of these conditions."

"I have connections."

"Don't try to use them. You'll cause difficulty for both of us if you do."

"Very well."

"I take that as a promise, Mr. Jasper."

"It's a promise I may not be able to keep. If I should happen to see them walking past my office building, I'll knock the hell out of—"

"It's a long way from Hibiscus Court to the Jasper building. However, I think they're still in the city. Otherwise Lennard wouldn't have asked permission for his bride to come and live in the court with him. There's another fact: Lennard has a job to keep."

"That's what he thinks," Jasper said. "As of tomorrow morning Lennard's name will be off the school payroll and the salary for the two weeks' notice he's entitled to will be mysteriously delayed or lost in the mails. The facts surrounding his dismissal will be available to any prospective employer. Let's see how romance thrives on a little adversity."

"Sometimes it does, Mr. Jasper."

Jasper refused to consider this. "It will be three years before Cleo comes into her fortune. I confidently predict that by that time Roger Lennard will be long gone and forgotten and Cleo's estate will have a conservator."

"Your second prediction may come true but I wouldn't bet on the first one."

"He will be gone and forgotten," Jasper repeated with grim satisfaction.

When the two men parted, Jasper didn't offer to shake hands. It was a bad sign, a symptom, Aragon thought, of the paranoia often afflicting rich men, that people who didn't agree with them were against them.

Aragon unlocked the door of his car. Donny Whitfield's morning escapade had taught him to take more sensible precautions against chewing gum in the trunk lock. The gum was still there. He was about to get into the car when he heard a soft, tentative voice from the other side of the eugenia hedge:

"Señor?"

He replied in Spanish. "What are you doing over there?"

"Waiting to talk to you. Most privately."

"All right, get in and we'll go to the end of the driveway. The Jaspers are probably waiting to hear my car leave."

She got into the front seat, a short, plump woman wearing what seemed to be several layers of dark clothing. She smelled of oregano.

He said, "You're Valencia?"

"Yes. Valencia Ybarra."

"I'm Tomas Aragon. I'm looking for Cleo."

"I know. I heard. I hear things they don't want me to. They think because I don't speak so good English I don't understand, so they ignore me like a dog."

He parked on the street below and turned off his headlights.

"It's not so good talking here. The police are always driving past. I'm afraid they might arrest us."

"What for?"

"They don't need a reason when you're Chicano in a rich neighborhood. Chicanos are suspicious characters. How about we go and get some pizza?"

"Pizza?"

"Pepperoni. The food they serve in the house is so tasteless I am always hungry. Are you hungry?"

"Yes." He couldn't remember eating dinner.

"The pizza parlor is nearby, only about five blocks. I'm not dressed to go in but you could go in and bring something out for me."

If pepperoni pizza was the asking price for some inside information, he was willing to pay it.

As they ate he thought of Donny Whitfield. The boy had had nearly twelve hours of non-diet by this time and had probably used every minute to advantage.

"So you hear things, Valencia?"

"Many."

"Why did Cleo run away?"

She was amazed by the question. "To get a man. Why not? That is natural. They would never allow her to get a man, especially the señor. He treated her like a little girl and she behaved like a little girl. But not always. Ho ho, not always."

"What's the 'ho ho' about?"

"I am thirsty. A large Coke would soothe my throat."

Aragon provided the large Coke and waited.

"The night before she left," Valencia said, "Ted came home. It was late, everybody was in bed. She and Ted got together."

"What do you mean, they got together?"

"You don't know? How old are you anyway?"

"All right, all right, I know. But Ted is her nephew. They're blood relatives."

"Ah yes, they make such a fuss about things like that in this country. Is it so odd, two young people going to bed together? But the fussing that went on when the señor discovered them, oh, oh, you wouldn't believe it. Ted was forced to leave in the middle of the night. And the next morning the señor and his wife screamed at each other all through breakfast. Such language."

"And you think that's why Cleo ran away?"

"She went to find a man. She liked that business with Ted. She's ready to get married and have children. In Mexico pretty soon she'd be an old maid."

The news about Ted and Cleo had caught Aragon by surprise but he had little doubt of its validity. It fitted in with Jasper's reluctance to have his wife questioned and with Ted's suspicious reaction to the phone call Aragon had made to the house that morning. He asked Valencia about the call.

"Ted was at my elbow telling me what to say. He pinched my arm so hard it left a bruise."

"Where was Mrs. Jasper at this time?"

"She went to the bank to get Ted the money he wanted and wasn't supposed to have. . . . That was you on the other end of the line?"

"Yes."

"You don't go to school with Ted."

"No."

"You tell lies."

"When I have to."

"That's no excuse. I hope you confess to the priest."

She was sucking noisily the last drops of Coke from the bottom of her cup.

He said, "Shall I drive you home now?"

"I haven't finished yet. There are still things to tell."

"All right. Go on."

"Perhaps another Coke?"

Another Coke was provided. She was clearly enjoying the scene—the food and drink, the attention, the activity going on around her—and seemed in no hurry to end it.

"I should come here more often," she said. "The Jasper house is so quiet, like someone died. I like a bit of noise, people laughing and music playing, even babies crying. Sometimes it's a relief to hear the dog barking or Trocadero mowing the lawn or clipping hedges."

"Quit stalling, Valencia."

"Do you think we could come here another time?"

"Maybe."

"That means no, doesn't it?"

"It probably does."

"Oh well, you're too young for me anyway. And too Anglo. You even look Anglo with those horn-rimmed glasses of yours. Who ever heard of a Chicano wearing horn-rimmed glasses? Most of them don't read."

"You're stalling again, Valencia. Get back to the subject, whatever it is."

93

"It's Ted, of course. You weren't the only one who telephoned him before he left the house. After lunch he had another call. I put him on and then I heard him say, 'All right, I'll be right there.' Those were his words: 'All right, I'll be right there.' "

"That doesn't sound very sinister."

"Maybe not, unless you know who the caller was, or you think you know. It was her voice, Cleo's."

"Cleo's?"

"Aha, surprised you, didn't I? You didn't believe me before when I said she liked that business with Ted. Now you've changed your mind, eh? She's young and hungry—why should she not eat?"

"Did you inform Mrs. Jasper about this phone call from Cleo or a girl you thought was Cleo?"

"Never. It would start another big fuss. They treat me like a dog, I behave like a dog, I say nothing."

"The rumor is that Ted has a number of girl friends. It would be quite natural for him to move in with one of them after being kicked out of his own house."

"The voice was Cleo's. She asked him to meet her someplace and he said all right, he would. His car was already packed with his clothes and things because he had to leave before his father got home. The señora stood at the door, waving goodbye and crying. Silly woman. What's there to cry about when a baby bird flies out of the nest? If he stayed on, now *that* would be good cause for crying."

"What time did Ted leave?"

"Between one-thirty and two."

He recalled the picture of Ted as a senior in his high school yearbook, a baby bird already out of the nest even then. "Did he seem happy about going?"

"Why not? He's a fine-looking young man with a fine car and money in his pocket. He's a bit on the heavy side for my taste. I prefer the lean type like you. Lean men are often stronger."

"I'm extremely weak," Aragon said.

He figured it was time to drive Valencia home.

He let her off at the bottom of the Jaspers' driveway. Through the trees he could see the house at the top of the hill. The main floor was dark but lights showed in some of the second-floor windows.

"If I were you, Valencia, I wouldn't mention any of this to the Jaspers. It will only increase their burden."

"It could very well increase mine too. They might fire me. Chicanos are blamed for everything."

"Things are changing."

"Not for me."

"You have a comfortable place to stay, don't you?"

"Yes."

"You have a room of your own, a radio and TV perhaps, regular meals."

"The meals are tasteless," she said. "And the room is lonely without a man. Perhaps you have an older brother? An uncle?"

"I come from a very small family of very weak men."

"Now you're making fun of me."

"I'd like to see you smile."

"I never smile. I have a crooked tooth at the front. Besides, who's there to smile at? Trocadero? He's over seventy. The grocery boy goes to high school and the garbage man is black as coal."

"When the right man comes along you'll smile without even thinking of your crooked tooth. And the right man won't even see it."

"What a liar you are," Valencia said, sounding pleased. "You'd better go see your priest."

9

Drawford's department store catered to the young ladies and the old money of the city's North Side. Located at the head of a recently constructed shopping mall, it was built in the style of the string of old missions along the southern California coast. There were differences. Its bell tower clanged the hours only when the store was open for business, the taped music was soft and secular except at Christmas, and the thickly carpeted floors were not meant for the bare feet of padres. Bare feet were not, in fact, allowed at all. There was a sign to that effect on each of the four entrance doors.

The credit department was on the third floor. Its manager was on vacation but the assistant manager agreed to see Aragon.

She was a young woman who looked as if she'd been born and brought up in the store itself, nurtured on the skinny sandwiches of its tearoom, coiffed in its beauty salon, clothed in its designer dresses, perfumed and made up in the cosmetics section, educated in the pages of its chic, glossy catalogues. Aragon would scarcely have been surprised if she'd introduced herself as Ms. Drawford.

"I'm Mrs. Flaherty," she said. "May I help you?"

Aragon gave her his card and she read it through jewel-trimmed glasses from the optometry department.

"Drawford's is always happy to welcome an attorney," she said with a well-practiced smile. "Especially if he's on our side."

"Thank you."

"What can we do for you?"

"I'm trying to find out if the holder of a certain credit card purchased anything here during the past week."

"I'm sorry but we cannot give out that information." It sounded like a line from Drawford's Training Manual for New Personnel.

"Does that mean under any circumstances, Mrs. Flaherty?"

"Almost any. It would be advisable if you'd wait for Mr. Illings to get back from his fishing trip in British Columbia. That will be in another week and a half."

"That might be a week and a half too late. This is really important."

Mrs. Flaherty threw away the manual. "Oh damn, I knew something like this was going to happen the minute he left. Right off the bat someone waltzes in, a lawyer yet, and asks for confidential information. What am I supposed to do?"

"Use your own judgment."

"Okay. What's the name of the credit card holder, the billing address and the number of the card?"

"Cleo Jasper. The bills are probably sent to her brother, Hilton Jasper, on Via Vista."

"And the number of the card?"

"I don't have it, sorry."

"I'd really like to know what this is all about."

"And I'd really like to tell you. But as any employee of Drawford's must realize, rules are rules."

"All right, I'll see what I can do. I'll have to get her credit card number from our files, then run it through the computer and see what comes out."

She was gone for five minutes, during which Aragon had time to examine her office. It was mostly chrome and glass, very neat and almost devoid of personal touches except for two small framed photographs on the desk, one of a baby and the other of a young man in football uniform who looked like Joe Namath. Drawford's would probably not approve of an assistant credit manager having a photograph of Joe Namath on her desk, so Aragon assumed the picture was of Mrs. Flaherty's husband, and the baby their joint effort.

Mrs. Flaherty returned carrying a sheet of paper. "The computer indicates that Miss Jasper made some purchases two days ago."

"What were they?"

"We don't know yet. When a purchase is made, the slip contains the name of the credit card holder and the number of the associate. When we check that number we'll have the name of the associate and thus the department in which she or he works."

"By 'associate' you mean sales clerk?"

"If you insist. Drawford's believes that *associate* sounds better and improves morale. Now then, we'll find out whether that associate is working today and after that you can do—well, whatever it is that people like you do."

"They work," Aragon said, ". . . and when do I get the names of the associates?"

"My secretary's checking that now."

The secretary turned out to be not a clone of Mrs. Flaherty but a close copy. She had the same hairdo and wore an almost identical expression and dress. She said that one of the numbers belonged to Mrs. deForrest of the shoe salon and the other to Miss Horowitz of the Better jewelry department. Miss Horowitz had sold Miss Jasper a set of rings and Mrs. deForrest had sold her two pairs of shoes.

This was Miss Horowitz's day off but Mrs. deForrest was on duty in the shoe salon, having clocked in at 9:07 that morning.

Mrs. deForrest was not a product of Drawford's catalogues or training manual. She looked like a grandmother who'd had to go back to work in order to pay her bills.

"Cleo Jasper," she said, frowning. "Let me think a minute. I'm pretty good at names."

While Mrs. deForrest thought, Aragon watched the other customers: a middle-aged woman surrounded by piles of boxes which indicated she was either hard to please or hard to fit, two teenagers pooling their finances to pay for a pair of sandals, an elegantly dressed woman in a wheelchair examining a display of matching shoes and handbags.

"Yes," Mrs. deForrest said. "Yes, I recall now. A young woman, who had trouble signing her name. In fact she didn't sign her first name. She used only the initial."

Aragon showed her one of the pictures Mrs. Jasper had given him of Cleo.

"Of course this is the girl," Mrs. deForrest said. "Why didn't you show it to me in the first place?"

"I thought she might have changed her appearance and seeing the picture would only put you off."

"Well, she did not change it. The picture's exactly her. Cute little thing. Bought a pair of Italian sandals with very high heels. She could hardly walk in them. She looked comical, like a little girl dressed up in her mother's clothes. I urged her to buy a more sensible pair of shoes for walking, with a special non-slip sole. We sell a lot of them to people who want to be sure of their footing on slippery surfaces. And that's especially important for someone in Mrs. Jasper's condition."

"Miss Jasper."

"Miss? Dear me, that's getting so common these days but I still can't help being shocked."

"What is common?"

"Going right ahead and having children without bothering to get married. Why, she looked barely out of high school and she had that eight-month waddle if I ever saw one. That's why the non-slip shoes were so important, to avoid a fall that might cause a premature birth."

"Would you take another look at this picture, Mrs. de-Forrest?"

"Sure." She studied the picture again, more carefully. "I certainly think it's the same girl. I wouldn't want to swear on a stack of Bibles. If I had to do that, swear to it in court or anything, I really couldn't. I'd hate to get involved in anything messy."

"So would I," Aragon said. But he knew he had.

Contacted by phone at her apartment, Miss Horowitz confirmed the sale of a pair of rings to Cleo Jasper. Sales were never brisk in the better jewelry department, Miss Horowitz explained, except when there was a special sale on such things as diamonds and jade, so individual customers were easy to recall. The girl had bought a set of wedding bands. The girl's band was too big for her but she said she would grow into it. She didn't want to wait for a special order. . . . "I don't wonder she was in a hurry. She was conspicuously pregnant."

"Was she happy about it?"

"Quite. In fact, very. I honestly can't understand the present generation. Can you?"

"No."

He understood even less Cleo's apparently imminent contribution to the next generation.

When Aragon reached the parking lot of his apartment

building he could hear a phone ringing from one of the open windows. He didn't hurry. If the ringing came from his apartment he couldn't reach the phone in time anyway. He locked his car, counting the rings of the phone automatically at first, then, as they continued, deliberately: ten . . . twelve . . . sixteen. . . . They stopped for about half a minute, then began again. When he went up the steps to the second floor he realized the ringing was coming from his own apartment.

He let himself in, breathing deeply to expel the sense of impending disaster he felt. The call must be very urgent or the ringing would have stopped at the usual six or seven.

He said, "Hello?"

"Mr. Aragon?"

"Yes."

"This is Rachel Holbrook. I'm in a café across the street. I saw your car drive up. I've been waiting for you."

"How did you know where to wait?"

"A girl in your office gave me your address and told me you usually came home at noon to pick up your mail in case there was a letter from your wife."

"They're a chatty group."

"A bit unprofessional, yes. Would you come over and have a cup of coffee with me? It's very important."

"About Cleo?"

"It's a related matter. Can you come?"

He didn't want to and she must have sensed it. Her voice hardened.

"You owe me one, Mr. Aragon. Don't you pay your debts?"

"When I know what they are."

"Come on over and I'll tell you about this one, such as how to pay it."

"All right."

She sat in the front booth, looking out of place in the

dingy blue-collar café with its cigarette-scarred tables and splitting vinyl seats. She wore a white-brimmed hat and a dark-red suit with white collar and cuffs. He didn't like the color, which reminded him not of burgundy or plums but of raw liver or yesterday's blood.

There was a glass of water in front of her, untouched. The water looked murky and the table was marked with the rings of other glasses from other meals.

"This isn't a nice place," she said abruptly.

"I didn't pick it."

"I've become spoiled. All through college I worked in joints like this and it didn't bother me. Now I feel—well, frightened, uneasy. Those men eating lunch at the counter, I'm sure they have no evil intentions toward me. And yet . . . and yet, perhaps they do."

"Their only intention is to eat their food." And keep it down, he added silently. "What's happened, Mrs. Holbrook?"

"Donny Whitfield has been missing since yesterday morning. That's the one you owe me, Mr. Aragon."

"I see."

"You don't appear surprised."

"No."

"He escaped in your car."

"I believe so."

"The evidence I have doesn't indicate any actual complicity on your part, Mr. Aragon. Just stupid negligence, leaving your car keys in the ignition. Nothing goes unnoticed around Holbrook Hall. One of our students saw the whole thing but she didn't report it until the search for Donny began last night. She had the make and model of your car, even the license number." Mrs. Holbrook took a sip of water. "Although the search was as quiet and unobtrusive as possible, I knew I'd have to make up some plausible story about Donny to stop the speculations. I told two of the key students of the school grapevine—key for key-hole—that Donny's father had decided to send him to a fat camp for the summer. So far, my version has been accepted."

"Does Mr. Whitfield know about Donny?"

"I was unable to reach him. He has a house in Palm Springs, a condominium near the harbor and a yacht moored at the marina, but he wasn't at any of those places."

A waiter approached the table and Mrs. Holbrook ordered a cup of coffee and Aragon a bowl of soup. He knew the soup came from a can and nothing much could be done to ruin it.

"Donny's a wild boy," Mrs. Holbrook said. "I had a great many misgivings about accepting him at the school. But he put on a good show during our initial talks. He was sweet, contrite, eager to please, ready to cooperate. I bought the whole act. His first violent rage came as a shock to me. I didn't report it to his father. Donny himself was the victim of violence. It was almost inevitable that he'd pass it on."

"He told me he was on probation. What for?"

"Assault with a deadly weapon."

"Then you'll have to call the police in on this."

"I will, of course. I'm stalling, trying to give him a chance to come back of his own accord. If he doesn't, his probation will be revoked and he'll be sent God knows where. I would like to prevent that. Donny's a victim. His father is what is politely called a wealthy playboy, meaning a rich man without discipline, morals or responsibility. His mother was a bit actress who took to booze and barbiturates and eventually overdosed when Donny was five. A succession of stepmothers and live-ins weren't much improvement."

"Where do I fit into this?" Aragon said. "You didn't go

to the trouble of coming here in order to discuss Donny Whitfield's case history."

"No, I didn't."

"The boy's escape is the one I owe you. How do you want it paid?"

"Let me state my position, not as a person, but as the head of a school which serves an important purpose in the community."

"Go ahead."

The soup arrived, overwatered and underheated, but Aragon ate it anyway while Mrs. Holbrook watched him with the ill-concealed irritation of someone who is not hungry.

"You pay me back," she said finally, "by keeping silent."

"About what?"

"Donny Whitfield. His disappearance is not yet generally known and I'd like to keep it that way as long as possible. He may come back of his own volition. Meanwhile something else has happened. Mr. Jasper has called a meeting of the board of directors for this afternoon at two o'clock at the school. Each member of the board contributes heavily to our endowment fund, so it doesn't function merely as an advisory committee. I wasn't invited as I usually am, and Mr. Jasper didn't tell me the reason for the sudden meeting, but I think something more is involved than just Cleo running away from home. My efforts to contact Roger Lennard have failed and I've begun to suspect the worst."

"What's your idea of the worst, Mrs. Holbrook?"

"What you mentioned as a possibility the first time we met, that Cleo and Roger are together somewhere. Even worse than worst, that Mr. Jasper has found out about it. Mr. Jasper has never called a meeting of the board before, in fact has seldom attended one. He must have discovered something linking Cleo and Roger, and he's going to blame the school for it."

"He didn't discover it," Aragon said. "I did."

"I can't believe it. Roger's not a bisexual, or a promiscuous homosexual. He's had the same lover ever since he came to town last December. I've seen him when he's come to pick Roger up at the school several times. A man about Roger's age, a muscle-beach type, evidently the macho partner in the marriage. That's what Roger called it—a marriage."

"Do you know his friend's name?"

"We were never introduced, but in our conversations Roger referred to him as Timothy."

Timothy North, of the pink bungalow and the exercise machine and the cock-and-bull story about a stranger coming into the bar with a lost basset hound. The story had been crazy enough to be true. And Aragon had accepted it because there seemed to be no reason for him to lie.

"One of the factors in my hiring Roger in the first place was his steady relationship with this man Timothy. Call it a marriage, a pair bond, whatever. They were like an ordinary couple searching for a house to buy which they could afford. Because of the strength of this relationship, I felt Roger could be completely trusted with both the male and female students. I'm at a loss to explain what could have happened."

"No one is asking you to explain."

"No?" She stared into the cup of coffee as though she could see its bitterness without bothering to taste it. "Do you know how the board of directors will regard this? They will question my judgment, my hiring practices, my character, perhaps even my sanity. The school will be found guilty, its administration, its faculty, its policies, all guilty as charged. They must not be given an additional count against me, like Donny's running away."

"'I don't intend to tell anybody, Mrs. Holbrook."

"Oh, they'll find out anyway, of course. But meanwhile

Donny might decide to return voluntarily. It's quite possible."

But her troubled eyes indicated she didn't think so. Neither did Aragon.

"It was a mistake to put him on that diet," Mrs. Holbrook said. "I argued with the dietitian about it but she insisted it would improve Donny's self-image if he lost some weight. It's frightening how logical theories and good intentions can blow up in your face. I wonder—I've often wondered—are the Donnys and Cleos worth the trouble they cause? Twenty years ago if I'd heard myself asking a question like that I would have been appalled. Now I simply grope for answers and come up with more questions. How many lives should be warped for the sake of one disturbed child? If it's true about Roger and Cleo, why in God's name didn't he have sense enough to realize what he was getting into and back out of it? Couldn't he see what a dismal future was in store for him?"

"Cleo will inherit a million dollars when she's twenty-five," Aragon said. "That might make his future less dismal."

"Roger doesn't care about money. His work, his books, his music, these are the things he values."

"A million dollars will buy a lot of books and music. Even if Cleo could be found mentally incompetent to handle her own affairs, once she's married to Roger he will be her guardian, not Jasper, no matter what legal maneuvers he goes through."

"You wouldn't be so cynical about Roger if you met him."

"I intend to do just that."

"I can't believe that Roger would—I just can't believe—"

"Yes, you can, Mrs. Holbrook," Aragon said. "You've already started."

He paid the bill and walked her back to her car, a black Seville parked about a block away. The front bumper overlapped the parking space marker by at least two feet, a fact that did not go unnoticed. A handwritten note pushed under the windshield wiper read *Lern To Park*. Although she smiled slightly as she crumpled the note in her hand she didn't look amused. To people in her profession reprimands were to give, not to take.

"I'd like to think quite a few of my pupils can spell better than this," she said dryly. "Well, thank you for your time, Mr. Aragon. I appreciate your promise to keep quiet about Donny Whitfield. Things are already bad enough. The Cleo story won't look very pretty in the newspaper: *School Counselor Elopes with Retarded Heiress.*"

"The local paper is usually more tactful than that."

"Not where Mr. Jasper is concerned. He's for oil-drilling in the channel. They stand opposed. They wouldn't pass up a chance like this to get at him, perhaps at me as well. Some people resent having a school like ours in their vicinity. They consider our students dangerous. They're not, of course."

Neither of them mentioned the name of the exception.

He told her he would be interested in hearing the outcome of the board of directors' meeting and wrote down on his card the telephone number of his apartment and of his office, which had a twenty-four-hour answering service.

As he watched her pull away from the curb he hoped her driving was a little better than her parking and a lot better than that of Mrs. Griswold, who'd returned the basset hound to the Jaspers.

He remembered his wild ride through the city streets following Mrs. Griswold to her tenant's bungalow to pay the reward money.

Timothy North must have laughed all the way to the bank.

10

Shortly before two o'clock the members of the board of directors began arriving. From the north windows of her office Mrs. Holbrook could have watched them, noting which ones had found time to come to a meeting so suddenly arranged. She stood instead at the south window, surveying the grounds of her school. She knew every square foot of its acreage, the tennis and basketball courts, the pool enclosed by an eight-foot chain-link fence with its gate double-padlocked, the picnic grounds, the corral and dog runs; she knew how much the new roof for the stable had cost; she knew the names of every horse and dog, of every shrub and tree on the property. It was her small kingdom and for thirty years she had lived in it and for it.

Tears stung her eyes and blurred her vision. Everything seemed to be moving, as if the first tremor of an earthquake had struck. There was a knock on the door. She blinked away the tears and said, "Come in."

A girl entered, carrying an oversized canvas tote bag with the name Gretchen printed on it. She was sixteen, large and sturdy, with a moon face and round eyes and the faint trace of a moustache.

"I came to clean," Gretchen said.

"You cleaned yesterday, Gretchen. Things haven't had a chance to get dirty."

"I see dirt that other people can't."

"All right. Go ahead."

The girl began her work at the bottom shelf of one of

the bookcases. She sat on the floor, removed a dustcloth from the tote bag and started wiping each book individually. She hummed tunelessly as she worked. The noise didn't bother Mrs. Holbrook. Gretchen was happy at these times and Mrs. Holbrook was happy for her.

Her gaze returned to the school grounds. A picnic was in progress and a group of boys was playing basketball, coached by their athletic director, Miss Trimble. A girl was working a quarter horse in the training ring but the pool and the tennis courts were empty. Only one student was using the playground. He was swinging on a tire suspended from a limb of a huge cypress tree.

His name was Michael and he was new and very quiet and Mrs. Holbrook was worried about him. She went down the hall and out the back door and crossed the lawn to the cypress tree. The boy didn't turn his head or indicate in any way that he was aware of her.

"Hello, Michael," she said. "Do you like swinging?"

His eyes were closed and he might have been asleep except for the movement of his legs.

"Have you had lunch, Michael?"

He made a sound that could have been yes or no. She was quite sure it was no. The dietitian had already discussed Michael's case with her. A problem eater given to hunger strikes, he was at least twenty pounds underweight.

"I have a bowl of very nice apples in my office," she said. "Or perhaps you and I could walk down to the grove and pick some oranges. Would you like that?"

He spoke without opening his eyes.

"I hate you."

"I don't hate you back, Michael. I think you and I can become good friends. Your mother's driving down to see you next month. Did you know that?"

"I hate you."

She felt the sting of tears again. She would have liked to

hate him back but . . . Instead, she wanted to hold him in her arms and comfort him. He was helpless and possibly hopeless. There was no apparent cause for his condition. He had loving parents, three sisters and a brother, all normal, and no history of childhood illnesses or accidents. He was probably, as one of the counselors had pointed out, the victim of the commonest and most mysterious cause of all, a failure of genetic programming, a fancy name for rotten luck. She tried to remember which counselor had said it. Perhaps it was Roger Lennard and perhaps he was talking about himself, not this quiet boy on the swing with his eyes closed to the world.

"You can't see anything unless you open your eyes, Michael," she said gently. "It's like being blind, and you wouldn't like to be blind, would you? . . . I know. I bet someone has glued your eyelashes together. Let's go to the tap over there and wash away the glue, and presto, your eyes will pop open again. How about it?"

"I hate you."

"That's okay. I'm not so crazy about me, either."

She turned and went back to her office, pausing only to pick up some bark that had peeled off the lemona eucalyptus tree and toss it in the trash bin. A failure in genetic programming. Rotten luck. She was almost sure now those were Roger's words and that he'd been talking about himself. Though he had never openly indicated dissatisfaction with his role in life, she sometimes sensed his uneasiness, his awareness that he was out of sync, out of tune.

In the office Gretchen was still at work on the bottom shelf of books, still humming, still happy. Mrs. Holbrook picked up the phone and called Roger's number as she had done a dozen times in the past two days. She was about to hang up when she heard the click of a receiver being lifted.

"Roger? Is that you, Roger?"

The only answer was a whimpering animal sound followed by the thud of something falling, or being thrown.

"Roger, it's Rachel Holbrook. Are you drunk? Answer me."

She waited for a full minute before hanging up. She felt dizzy with anger, days, weeks, years of anger, at the Rogers and Cleos and Donnys and Michaels and boards of directors, years of anger she had never shown, never even realized she felt.

She spoke as quietly and as calmly as possible to the girl sitting on the floor. "I have an important errand, Gretchen. Perhaps we'd better postpone the rest of the cleaning to another day."

"No, I can't. Everything's terribly dirty. It's going to take me six months to finish up."

"I need your cooperation, Gretchen. My secretary had to go to the dentist. When he returns I want you to give him a message for me. Can you do that?"

"No. I'm very busy."

"Gretchen, for God's sake—"

"You told us not to swear," Gretchen said. "God is a dirty word."

The carport beside Space C of Hibiscus Court was occupied by a car Mrs. Holbrook recognized as Roger Lennard's, a red Pinto station wagon with Utah license plates.

She stopped her Seville behind it and was about to get out when a man came hurrying toward her. He was an old man, so brown and wrinkled he looked as though he'd been hung out to dry in the California sun like a string of chili peppers.

"You can't stop there, lady," he said.

"Why not?"

"These are single units, one parking space apiece, no exceptions." The old man removed his straw hat. "My

111

name's Abercrombie. I make sure the rules are followed."

"I'm in a hurry."

"Everybody's in a hurry. When everybody's in a hurry nobody gets anywhere. It's like all the people wanting to drive in the fast lane when the other lanes are open."

"Where do I leave my car?"

"You can go back to the street or you can follow this road to the guest parking lot at the rear."

She went back to the street. She had the impression that Mr. Abercrombie's rules would cover every inch, every nook and cranny, every leaf and blade of grass on the premises. When she returned he had disappeared.

She knocked on Roger Lennard's door and said in the voice she reserved for students who were being deliberately malicious, "Roger, it's Rachel Holbrook. I want to talk to you. Open this door."

If there was any response she couldn't hear it above the sounds of traffic on the street and in the air.

She knocked again, waited, then tried the door. It was locked. She'd come prepared for that. Now and then one of the students would lock himself in a dorm or lavatory or classroom and she would have to call in a locksmith to extricate him. After a number of these occasions the locksmith had provided her with a piece of metal, one of the tools of his trade called a picklock, and taught her how to use it. She carried it in her purse as casually as she did her wallet and lipstick. She used it now expertly, her body screening her movements from the possible gaze of Mr. Abercrombie.

The door opened. The first thing she saw was a kitchen table containing a salt shaker, a bottle of ketchup and a typewriter. There was a sheet of paper in the typewriter and a white envelope beside it. The kitchen chair was overturned and the telephone was on the floor beside it. It was a child's phone in the form of Mickey Mouse and she couldn't imagine Roger owning such a thing unless it had been given to him by a practical joker.

"Roger?"

She took a tentative step into the room. It was only then that she saw him lying on his side on a couch, his partly open mouth revealing bright red stains.

She forced herself to go over and touch his forehead. It was warm, but not warm enough. She picked up the telephone and called the emergency number printed on the front of it. Then she righted the kitchen chair and sat down to wait for the police and paramedics. She knew what the red stains in his mouth meant: There was nothing that could be done for Roger except by experts.

Even in the dim light she could make out the words on the page in the typewriter.

She picked up the white envelope and saw with a shock that it was addressed to her at Holbrook Hall. It was ready to be mailed, sealed and stamped with an extra stamp because of its bulk. Impulsively, without even thinking of any consequence of her action, she put the envelope in her purse. Then she called one of the numbers Aragon had written on his card.

He answered on the second ring. "Yes?"

"This is Rachel Holbrook," she said. "I'm at Roger Lennard's place. I think he's dead."

"Dead?"

"Yes. Pills."

"How did you get in?"

"I used a picklock."

"Surely you know that's illegal."

"Yes."

"What else have you done?"

"I took an envelope from the table. It was addressed to

me, sealed and stamped. I consider it my property."

"What you consider and what the police consider may be quite different. You've called them, haven't you?"

"Yes."

"Put the letter back. Stay cool. I'll be right over."

He hung up.

She opened her purse to put the letter back, then closed it again. It was her property, Roger wanted her to have it, no one had any right to take it from her. Clutching the purse under her arm, she went out the door into the afternoon sun.

Mr. Abercrombie was leaning against the hood of Roger's car, watching her.

"I saw what you did," he said. "Picked the lock like an old pro."

"I had to. I thought he might be drunk."

"And is he?"

"No. I think he's dead."

Abercrombie made a snorting little noise. "You women are always exaggerating. A man takes a drink, he's drunk. He lies down for a nap, he's dead."

"I called the police and paramedics."

"For crying out loud, you crazy lady. What did you do that for? Why didn't you come to me? We can't have police and paramedics cluttering up the property for no reason except your imagination."

Two sounds were audible now: the full-scale siren of the police and the two-note electronic whelper of the paramedics.

"Crazy lady," Abercrombie said again. But he unfolded a canvas chair for her to sit on and began fanning her with his straw hat.

"Mr. Lennard had a row," he said. "You know, a quarrel. A man came to see him around lunchtime and I could hear their voices real loud until someone closed the windows. I saw the man leave, walk toward the street. He was a big fellow, heavyset, wearing a light gray suit and a Panama hat. Of course there's no chance of foul play or anything like that," he added anxiously. "Is there?"

"I can't answer that."

"Do you think I should tell the police about Mr. Lennard quarreling with that man?"

"Yes."

"Should I tell him about you picking the lock to get in?"

"No," Mrs. Holbrook said. "I'll tell them myself."

The paramedics arrived, four young men so quick and precise that their movements seemed choreographed. Abercrombie held the door open for them and they all went inside, filling the tiny room to capacity. People were already coming out of the other housing units, some curious, some frightened, some annoyed. They were quiet, listening to the paramedics' radio.

"This is Medic Two calling Santa Felicia Hospital. . . . We have a cardiac arrest, a man about thirty, no pulse, no respiration. . . . We're applying CPR, no luck so far. . . . We have him now on the scope, getting only a straight line. . . . Adrenalin intravenous started. . . . We're moving right out. . . ."

Roger was carried out, strapped to a stretcher. In the sunlight Mrs. Holbrook saw what she had missed previously: that his right eye and the whole right side of his face were badly swollen and discolored.

The police arrived as the emergency vehicle was pulling away, two black-and-whites and an unmarked car. The man who got out of the unmarked car looked like an ordinary middle-aged businessman on his way to his job at a bank or insurance office. He introduced himself to Abercrombie as Lieutenant Peterson, while three of the other men went inside.

"*She* discovered him," Abercrombie said, pointing to Mrs. Holbrook. "I don't know her. I never saw her before. She picked the lock. Go ahead, ask her."

"What is your name, sir?"

"Abercrombie."

"I'd like your full name and address, please."

Abercrombie told him and the lieutenant wrote down the information on a note pad.

"And the victim's name, please?"

"Victim?" Abercrombie repeated. "How do you know he's a victim?"

"Well, he was certainly the victim of something or we all wouldn't be here. Right?"

"His name was Roger Lennard."

"And his occupation?"

"A schoolteacher, something like that. He didn't call it a schoolteacher."

"Mr. Lennard was one of the counselors at my school," Mrs. Holbrook said.

"And your name is?"

"Rachel Holbrook."

"Address?"

"I live at the school, Holbrook Hall. Mr. Lennard called in sick a few days ago and I've been trying to get in touch with him on a certain matter. When I couldn't, I drove down here to see him, thinking he might be quite sick."

"Or drunk," Abercrombie said. "But *I* knew he couldn't be drunk. He was a Mormon—they're not supposed to drink. He wasn't sick, either. He was messing around with some girl, told me he was going to be married and wanted to bring the bride here until they could find a nice apartment. This is a single unit, see, and we don't allow—"

"You and I will talk later, Mr. Abercrombie," the lieutenant said. "I'd like to question Mrs. Holbrook alone for a few minutes, if you don't mind."

They sat in the back seat of Lieutenant Peterson's car. He closed the windows and turned on the air-conditioner.

"I called my lawyer," Mrs. Holbrook said. "I believe I should wait for him before answering any questions."

"That's your privilege, ma'm."

There was a silence. It didn't seem to bother the lieutenant. He leaned back and closed his eyes, as if he'd been waiting for a chance to take a nap.

"I've never been in a situation like this before," she said.

He didn't find the statement interesting enough to make him open his eyes.

"I mean, this sort of thing doesn't happen to a woman like me."

"Women like you don't usually go around picking locks either."

"I've never done it before except at school when I've had to free some student who'd been locked in a room."

"What did you use?"

"A picklock."

"Show it to me."

She opened her purse, taking no pains to hide the large envelope from Roger's kitchen table. It bore no sender's name or address; there was nothing to connect it with its source. She showed him the picklock.

"This belongs in a burglar's tool kit," he said, "not a lady's handbag."

"I gave you my reason for having it and my reason for using it. When you're trying to extricate a wildly hysterical child from a locked room you don't question the legality of what or how you do it. You just do it. On the last occasion it was a girl, fifteen. She wasn't hysterical. She was uncon-

117

scious from an overdose of Seconal. Her mouth and tongue and throat were bright red the way Roger's were. The girl lived. I don't think Roger will."

"Why not?"

"I've had some experience with death. Roger's body was already cooling." Her voice shook in spite of her efforts to control it. "I'm—I was very fond of Roger. His work with the students was so positive, he emphasized what they had, not what they didn't have. He gave them a sense of identity."

"What about his identity?"

"I can't answer that."

"You've done pretty well so far."

He gave her back the picklock and she returned it to her purse.

"Was Mr. Lennard depressed lately?" he said.

"No."

"Did he say anything to you about getting married?"

"No."

"Did you know he was having a love affair?"

"Yes."

"Were you acquainted with the girl?"

"It wasn't a girl."

She could see Aragon's old Chevvy trying to get into the road that bisected the court. A patrolman waved him away and he backed up into the street.

"What's his name?" the lieutenant said.

"Whose name?"

"The man you just recognized."

"He's my lawyer, Tomas Aragon."

"Never heard of him."

"I never heard of him either until a few days ago," she said. "As a matter of fact, he doesn't even know yet that he's my lawyer."

"You have surprises for everyone, Mrs. Holbrook."

"I've been getting quite a few myself lately."

"Well, let's see how Mr. Aragon reacts to his new client."

The lieutenant helped her out of the car and they stood waiting for Aragon's approach. After the shade and coolness of the air-conditioned car the sun was blinding and the heat oppressive, but the lieutenant neither blinked nor unbuttoned his coat. He said to Aragon, "Mrs. Holbrook's lawyer, I presume?"

Aragon acknowledged his sudden appointment with a somewhat baffled smile and the two men exchanged names as they shook hands.

"Mrs. Holbrook and I have just concluded a pleasant little chat," the lieutenant said. "She has an interesting new hobby you should discuss with her some time. You might want to encourage her to take up something more conventional, like needlepoint."

Aragon looked at Mrs. Holbrook. "You told him about the picklock?"

"I had to. Abercrombie saw me use it."

"You wouldn't make a very good criminal, Mrs. Holbrook."

"Don't sell her short," the lieutenant said. "She may be telling me a little so I won't ask her for a lot." Then to Mrs. Holbrook: "I'd like you to stick around for a while until I talk to Mr. Abercrombie and get a report from the hospital on Mr. Lennard. Does that suit you?"

"It will have to, I guess."

"You guessed right."

He didn't offer them the use of his car to wait in, so they walked back and sat on a bus stop bench under an oak tree.

"Did you tell him I was your lawyer?" Aragon asked.

"Yes. Aren't you?"

"I don't know. If anything comes up which makes you and Mr. Jasper adversaries, my prior commitment is to him."

"Nothing has come up. Perhaps nothing will."

"I'd like to find out a little bit more about what I'm getting into. Did you put the envelope back as I asked you to?"

"No."

"No? That's it, no?"

"That's it."

He said a word in Spanish that he hadn't spoken since he was a teenager.

She looked at him curiously. "So what does that mean?"

"It means, what am I going to do with this dame and how did I get into a crazy situation like this?"

"It means all that?"

"To me it does."

"You'll have to spell it for me some time."

"I don't think so," Aragon said. "Where's the envelope now?"

"In my purse."

"Will you let me see it?"

"What good would that do? It's still sealed. I don't intend to open it until I'm alone."

"What have you got to lose?"

"It's what Roger has to lose that concerns me. There might be something in here that, if he survives, he wouldn't want people to know, things he might regret having written. The envelope is full and carries an extra stamp. There's more to it than just a simple suicide note."

"It may be more than just a simple suicide," Aragon said. "When I came in I heard a couple of policemen talking about an attack. Someone hit Roger a hard blow on the right side of his face. His hands were unmarked, so apparently he didn't put up much of a fight, either because he was knocked unconscious or because he didn't want to."

"Abercrombie told me Roger had a visitor around lunchtime, a big man wearing a gray suit and Panama hat. Abercrombie heard them quarreling."

"Timothy North is a big man, and in view of Roger's impending marriage he and Roger had a lot to quarrel about. But I somehow doubt that he owns any suits. They're not part of his life-style. . . . Mr. Jasper is also a big man."

"Yes."

"He probably owns a couple of dozen suits."

"Very likely."

"What's more, he's left-handed."

"What does that have to do with it?"

"The injuries to Roger's face were on the right side, one of the policemen said."

She touched her own face as though it hurt and she expected to find it bleeding. "Roger—Mr. Jasper—these are not violent people. How did all this happen to them? And to me? I'm a respectable woman. I don't go around breaking into people's houses or picking up things I'm not supposed to touch. Yet I did."

"It's not too late to correct one of those mistakes. Return the letter."

"It's my property."

"As long as it was on Roger Lennard's table, it belongs to him. If he had posted it, it would be yours on delivery."

He didn't realize her intention until she was already in the street, darting between the cars. She must have been sixty or more, but she moved with the speed of a natural athlete and luck was with her. He didn't catch up with her

121

until the letter was in the mailbox, beyond the reach of everyone except the U.S. Postal Service.

"Roger intended to mail it," she said calmly. "I simply did it for him."

They returned to Hibiscus Court, walking in silence like strangers. The lieutenant was sitting in the front seat of his unmarked car, talking on a radiotelephone. He got out when he saw them coming.

His face remained impassive but he sounded rather amused. "You two look as if you've been playing games. A little hot for that, isn't it?" He didn't wait for an answer. "One of my men tells me you talked for a while at the bus stop, then Mrs. Holbrook suddenly dashed across the road and mailed something in the postbox. Is that right, Mrs. Holbrook?"

"Quite right," she said. "I remembered a letter I'd forgotten to post earlier."

"Memories like that pop up at the darnedest times, don't they? I mean, one minute you're sitting calmly talking to your lawyer and the next minute you're tearing across the road waving your purse to stop traffic."

"Things happen like that sometimes."

"Was it an important letter?"

"It was to me."

"Don't you have a secretary who handles that sort of chore?"

"He had to go to the dentist."

Because it was true it sounded true. He let the subject drop. To Aragon he said, "By the way, I didn't ask you how you managed to arrive here so fast. You got ESP? Listen to police calls?"

"I answer my telephone."

"Oh, never mind. I don't expect the truth anyway. I

haven't met a lawyer yet who told the truth the first time around."

"I'm sorry your experience has been so limited."

"That could be taken as a hostile remark."

"Yours wasn't very friendly either, lieutenant."

"Maybe not, but this is my show. You're the guest. When the time comes and it's your show I'll be just as polite as I have to be."

"I look forward to that."

The lieutenant returned his attention to Mrs. Holbrook. "Is this your first visit to Mr. Lennard's place?"

"Yes."

"Abercrombie tells me Lennard had another visitor around lunchtime."

"He told me that too."

"Can you guess who it might have been? Any ideas on the subject?"

"His description was very vague."

"That's not an answer to my question, Mrs. Holbrook. You said previously you were fond of Roger Lennard, very fond—I believe that was how you phrased it. If you were all that fond of him, you must know something about his private life."

"We had many conversations, but they were mostly about his work with the students."

"Do you know his friends?"

"Some of them."

"One in particular?"

"I knew Roger had one in particular but I wasn't personally acquainted with him. I only saw him when he came to pick Roger up at school occasionally."

"What's his name?"

"Timothy North."

"Is he locally employed?"

"He's a bartender. He's not in Roger's social class at all. I can't understand how the two of them—"

"Where does he tend bar?"

Mrs. Holbrook appealed to Aragon. "Do I have to answer all these questions?"

"He'll get the answers anyway," Aragon said. "If you save him time he might save you trouble."

"It's called Phileo's," Mrs. Holbrook said. "I believe it's a—well, a strange place. I'm sure Roger didn't go there habitually. He might have dropped in now and then. But Roger was a very idealistic young man."

"You keep referring to him in the past tense, Mrs. Holbrook."

"I'm sorry. I wasn't aware of doing it."

"You happen to be correct. Roger never regained consciousness. They've pulled the plugs."

She stood very straight and stiff. The lieutenant had seen other people do this when they were stretched too taut and getting ready to snap. "Let's stop the questioning for now."

"My God," she said. "What if I had come sooner? Could I have saved him? What if—"

"Look, this job is tough enough without the what-ifs. You go home and take a stiff drink. Or a couple of aspirin. To each his own."

"Did he kill himself?"

"He might have had a little help. However, there was a piece of paper in his typewriter that might have been the beginning of a suicide note. But we have no proof that it was or that he wrote it. You go home," he repeated. "Hit the booze or the aspirin and take a rest."

"I don't want—"

"You don't want," the lieutenant said. "But *I* want. Good day, Mrs. Holbrook."

* * *

She refused Aragon's offer to drive her back to the school, but she let him walk her to her car which she'd left at a gas station. She didn't move like the woman who'd run across the street to post the letter. Her gait was slow and awkward, as if she had, within the hour, grown years older and pounds heavier. She rested her head against the steering wheel for a moment before putting the keys in the ignition.

"Are you sure you can make it?" Aragon said.

"I have to," she said simply. "This has just been a preliminary event. The main bout's coming up now."

The scarcity of cars in the Privileged Parking zone made it apparent that the board of directors' meeting was over. She expected nothing further for the present than an informal note or a message from her secretary. Instead, her secretary had gone home and Hilton Jasper was sitting in the office, waiting.

In spite of the NO SMOKING PLEASE sign on her desk and the absence of ashtrays, he was smoking a cigarette. When she entered he crushed the cigarette in the wastebasket with obvious reluctance and rose to his feet.

"I've been waiting for you"—he consulted his wristwatch —"for over an hour."

"Punching a time clock isn't part of my job. This is my private office. Who let you in?"

He indicated the girl Gretchen, who was in the opposite corner of the room, still dusting books but no longer humming. "She's not much of a talker but she's a very good worker. I could use her in my business."

Gretchen gave no real sign that she heard or understood or cared, but she increased her pace and Mrs. Holbrook knew she had done all three.

She said, "You'd better stop for the day, Gretchen."

"I'm not finished."

"If you finish all the books today, you won't have any left to do tomorrow."

"I can do them again."

"That's nonsense, Gretchen. Now you hurry along and get into your swimsuit. It's almost pool time. You're such a strong swimmer, the timid students need your good example. Then afterwards maybe John will let you help him clean the pool."

The girl hesitated. She wanted to stay and dust the rest of the books but she also wanted to set a good example. Then suddenly she made up her mind, stuffed all the dustcloths into the tote bag and trudged across the room and out into the hall.

Mrs. Holbrook closed the door behind her and bolted it. "I suspect Gretchen of being one of the main stems of the school grapevine. By dinnertime everyone in the school will know that Cleo's brother was in my office and that he broke the no-smoking rule."

"She doesn't know I'm Cleo's brother."

"That's what you think. There are very few secrets around here. It's often wise to act as if every room was bugged." Though the smell of smoke was making her slightly ill, she closed the three windows that were open, then went back and sat at her desk, her hands folded in front of her. "Did the directors reach a conclusion?"

"Yes. In the best interest of the school, you are to ask Roger Lennard for his immediate resignation."

"That won't be easy."

"It might be simpler than you think."

"Indeed?"

"He won't be surprised, believe me. He's expecting it. I talked to him late this morning. He refused to admit he'd done anything wrong. In fact, he wouldn't even tell me where Cleo is. He lied, said he didn't know. I tried friendly persuasion to get the truth out of him. When that didn't work I hit him. He still wouldn't drop his injured innocence act, so I hit him again. He didn't even have guts enough to fight back."

"Roger didn't believe in violence."

"Well, maybe he does now." But the satisfaction in his voice had undertones of guilt. "I haven't hit anyone since I was a kid."

"Really? I hope you didn't hurt your hand. I notice you've been keeping it in your pocket. Let me see."

He took his left hand out of his pocket and she saw with pleasure it was almost as swollen and discolored as Roger's face.

She feigned surprise. "My goodness. Does it hurt?"

"Yes."

"You should have this examined."

"I haven't time to see a doctor."

"I didn't mean a doctor. I meant the police."

"Police? Are you telling me that little pipsqueak called the police because I hit him, after what he did to my sister, enticed her away from home, seduced her with promises—"

"No, that little pipsqueak didn't call the police," she said quietly. "I did."

"You did? Why?"

"I was the one who found him dead. I phoned the police and then Aragon."

For a few moments he was stunned and speechless. Then: "I didn't hit him that hard. I swear I didn't."

"Don't swear it to me. I have no jurisdiction."

"It's impossible to kill a man with your fist unless you're a professional boxer."

"Perhaps you missed your calling, Mr. Jasper."

Deliberately, almost maliciously, she withheld the information about the pills.

"Another tenant heard you quarreling with Roger and saw you leave," she said. "From his description and my own background knowledge I suspected it was you. But I didn't tell the police. Perhaps I would have if I'd been absolutely sure."

"Now that you're sure, what are you going to do?"

"Nothing. I expect you to do it yourself. Just phone and inform them that you hit Roger twice with your fist because he intended to marry, or had already married, your sister. Does that sound to you like a good story?"

"Not when you put it like that, when you leave out all the details."

"The details will come out later."

"For God's sake," he said, "I never meant—"

"That's irrelevant, isn't it?" She took a certain pleasure in watching him suffer. "The policeman I talked to this afternoon was a Lieutenant Peterson. I asked him what if I'd come sooner, and he stopped me. He said his job was tough enough without the what-ifs. Well, mine is tough enough without the I-never-meants."

"I went there only to reason with him. But he wouldn't be reasonable."

"If you're setting out to hit all the people who aren't reasonable, you're going to be a very busy man, Mr. Jasper."

"I didn't intend to kill him."

"Perhaps you didn't," she said. "He took some pills also. The actual cause of death won't be known until after an autopsy."

"Damn you, why didn't you tell me about the pills sooner?"

"Because I don't like bullies," she said. "And Roger was my friend."

11

Frieda spent the afternoon sorting through clothes and bric-a-brac and books to be donated to the Assistance League rummage sale. The clothing would be sent to the cleaners, the bric-a-brac washed or polished, the books dusted. She carefully avoided Cleo's room and Ted's. Ted's would be half-empty and Cleo's exactly the way she'd left it when she walked away with the dog.

The house was quiet and orderly without the two of them. Each hour came in a neat little package and piled up in corners unopened.

When Hilton arrived home for dinner she went downstairs to meet him.

"You're late," she said.

"I can tell time."

"Oh, we're in a mood, are we? You must have had a bad day."

"It was—interesting."

"That's more than mine was." She noticed his hand when he put his hat away in the hall closet. "What's the matter with your hand?"

"I hurt it."

"That's obvious. Let me take a look at it."

"Stop fussing. It doesn't suit you. Is dinner ready?"

It was ready. Cook had left some time ago and Lisa, the college girl who did the serving, was waiting in the kitchen. Someone—the cook? Valencia? Lisa?—had removed one or two of the extension boards of the dining room table, so it was smaller and appeared less deserted.

"If you're going to have difficulty handling a soup spoon with your right hand," Frieda said, "we can skip that course and go on to the salad."

"Get rid of the girl."

"What do you mean, get rid of her? Fire her?"

"Tell her we won't need her for tonight."

"Why?"

"I have something important to discuss with you in private."

"That sounds ominous. I don't like it. You're frightening me, Hilton."

"I can't help it."

"Is it about Cleo?"

"It's about me."

Lisa came in wearing her usual uniform: skintight jeans and T-shirt partly covered by an apron. She carried two bowls of soup, hot consommé floating sprigs of parsley on lemon rafts.

Frieda spoke in the too-bright voice she used as a cover-up. "Lisa, we've decided to have dinner alone tonight. You're free to leave."

Lisa put the soup bowls on the table in a manner that clearly indicated her displeasure. "I don't want to leave just yet. My boyfriend's not picking me up until eight o'clock."

"Where is he now?"

"The university library."

"Suppose you go and meet him. I'll give you five dollars for cab fare."

"That might not cover it and I'm broke."

"All right. Ten dollars."

"I still think it'd be simpler if I just stayed and served dinner as usual. A cab might get caught in a traffic jam. Or

Brent might finish his term paper early and we'd miss each other. I don't see why I can't sit quietly in the kitchen and watch television until Brent comes."

"I don't want to hear any television sounds coming out of the kitchen," Jasper said. "And I don't want any dining room sounds going into the kitchen. Have I spelled that out clearly enough for you?"

"Okay, okay. But I don't like having my plans screwed up like this."

"Here." He took a twenty-dollar bill from his wallet and shoved it at her. She stared at it a moment before accepting it. Then she folded it and tucked it into the rear pocket of her jeans. "I see you hurt your hand."

"Yes. Good night."

She phoned for a cab in the kitchen, speaking in a very loud, distinct voice to make sure they overheard. Then she went out the back door, slamming it behind her.

"Twenty dollars was too much," Frieda said.

"I didn't have a ten."

"You could have asked me."

"I could have, yes." *I could have . . . I never meant . . . what if . . .* Useless phrases belonging only to the past.

"What happened to your hand?"

"I hit a man."

"Oh, I don't believe it. You'd never do anything so primitive."

"Well, I did."

"What on earth for?"

"I wanted to make him tell me where Cleo is. I was sure he knew. She probably went directly to him the morning she left here. He refused to admit anything."

"You should have tried to bribe him. God knows that's not above you. We just had an example of it a minute ago."

"I wanted to hit him."

131

"That's always been the governing principle of your life. You wanted to do something, so you did it. . . . Do you want to eat your soup? If you don't, I'll take it back to the kitchen and we'll go on with the rest of the meal."

He looked at her bitterly. "There's no sympathy in you, is there, Frieda?"

"I'm reserving mine for the man who was hit."

"Don't waste your time. He's dead."

She tried to cover her alarm with a show of cynicism. "If this is one of your attempts to build yourself a macho image, forget it."

"I'll have to go to the police. I've been trying to get in touch with some of the company's lawyers but they're in Washington or L.A. or Sacramento. One is even hunting capercaillie in Scotland. They're everyplace but here. And they're not accustomed to dealing with cases like this anyway. It's a criminal matter."

"Roger Lennard," she said. "You killed Roger Lennard?"

"I'm not sure. He took some pills. Maybe he'd already taken them when I arrived. He made no attempt to fight back. I thought it was because he didn't have the guts, but maybe he was already dying. We have to wait for the results of an autopsy."

"How long will that take?"

"I don't know."

She sat twisting the soup spoon around and around between her fingers as though she was trying to wring its neck. "Chalk another one up to Cleo. She'll beat us all before she's through."

"Don't blame Cleo. It's my fault. Cleo wouldn't hurt a fly."

"No, she wouldn't hurt a fly. Or a dog or a horse. But what about the rest of us? We're the ones who get our wings pulled out, our paws stepped on."

"Please, let's not argue about Cleo. We have to decide what to do next."

"We? You mean I now have a part in the decision making?"

"You always did."

He was down and she would have liked to kick him a few more times to make sure he remembered after he got up again. But she was a reasonable woman with a keen sense of survival. He was down. That was enough.

"Give me the whole picture," she said. "You knocked at his door. Was it locked?"

"Yes."

"Did you tell him who was there?"

"Yes."

"And he unlocked the door and let you in?"

"Yes, right away. I had the peculiar feeling that he might even have been expecting me. He seemed almost resigned. He knew who I was, of course. Cleo probably talked about me to him the way she does to everyone."

"All right, he let you in. Then what?"

Her husband stared into his soup bowl. The little lemon raft with its cargo of parsley had floated to one side as if his breath had provided enough wind to move it. "He lives— lived—in a mobile home, a very small one where everything is wall-to-wall. There was a typewriter on the table, I remember, and a magazine on the couch. I asked him right away where Cleo was and he claimed he didn't know, that she'd walked out on him. He talked very slowly and calmly and that made me even angrier. I began to yell at him. One of the neighbors overheard me and reported it later to the police."

"When you hit him, did he fall down?"

"No. I hit him again."

"Then did he fall down?"

"No."

"How could you have killed him when he wasn't even knocked over by the force of the blows?"

"The effects of head injuries aren't always immediately apparent."

"But he was still standing up when you left?"

"Yes."

"Then the chances are that you had nothing to do with his death?"

"I made it clear to him that he didn't have much of a future in this town or in his profession or with Cleo. If that caused him to take an overdose of pills, then I have some moral responsibility for his death."

"A man doesn't commit suicide because of a few words spoken in anger. He may have been planning it for weeks, months, even years. He had many personal problems, according to Aragon." She paused. "What about Aragon? He might be able to help you."

"He's too young and inexperienced."

"At least he's not hunting capercaillie in Scotland," she said sharply. "Whatever the hell capercaillie is. Shall I call him?"

"If you like."

"If *I* like? What I'd like is a nice peaceful life without a husband who goes around slugging people."

She had hit him once too often while he was down. He was getting up now, and it showed in his face and his voice.

"The person I should have slugged is you, Frieda."

"It's a bit late for that. It would cost you too much, especially where it hurts, in the pocketbook."

"You intend to leave me, don't you?"

"If Cleo comes back, yes. I can't face another year like the past fourteen."

"Have things been that bad?"

"Worse. You don't realize that because you were away most of the time, at the office or at meetings out of town, while I was stuck at home watching her every minute, trying to teach her to talk properly and to read, looking after the succession of stray animals and birds she dragged home only to lose interest in them almost immediately, the way she lost interest in the dog Zia. She took him with her that morning and then she must have simply left him somewhere, forgot all about him."

"Why do our conversations always revert to Cleo?"

"Because she's been the focus of our lives, not you or I or Ted."

He said, "Here I am, in serious trouble, sitting in front of a bowl of cold soup, across the table from a wife who hates me, talking about a sister who ran away from me."

"At least we can take care of the cold soup part."

She carried the soup bowls back to the kitchen and returned with two plates of salad. "I repeat the question, Hilton. Shall I call Aragon? You don't have to take his advice, just see what he has to say."

"Go ahead."

"You might want to do it yourself."

"No. You handle these things very well, Frieda. It's one of your talents."

She used the wall phone in the kitchen. There was no answer from Aragon's apartment, so she left a message with the answering service at his office for him to call back. She saw the headlights of a car coming up the driveway and she thought at first what a nice coincidence it was, to have Aragon show up at the very time she was trying to get in touch with him. But as she listened she knew the car couldn't be his. The engine sounded too quiet and smooth.

She went to the front door and opened it at the first ring of the chime. The overhead light that switched on automatically when the door opened revealed a tall middle-aged man with a deeply tanned face and bright, expressionless eyes that reminded her of Cleo's.

"Mrs. Hilton Jasper?"

"Yes."

"You shouldn't open the door like that without first asking who is there."

"All right, who is here?"

"Lieutenant Peterson of the Police Department."

"This is an inconvenient time to receive you," she said coolly. "We're in the middle of dinner."

"Really? Funny thing, I was in the middle of dinner myself when the desk sergeant played me a tape of a message that had just come in from a woman. Sounded like a girl, actually. It seems she'd been listening to the six o'clock news and heard about the death of a man she knew, Roger Lennard. Is that name familiar to you?"

"Vaguely."

"Perhaps your husband might find it less vague."

Her response was to open the door a little farther to allow him to step inside. When she closed it again the overhead light went off and Lieutenant Peterson's face was in shadow. It looked better that way, more expressive, kinder, with the disturbing brightness of his eyes obscured.

"Let's not beat around the bush, Lieutenant," she said. "We've called our attorney and until he arrives my husband isn't going to make any statement."

"That's fine. I'll wait."

"I'm not sure when he's coming. I left a message with his answering service but he may not even get it tonight."

"I'll still wait. I presume you have a spare bedroom."

She let out a gasp of surprise.

"Now, now, don't get shook. That was just a little joke to lighten up the atmosphere."

136

"It wasn't very successful."

"Many of my jokes aren't. Win a few, lose a few. I'd like to see Mr. Jasper, all jokes aside."

"As I told you, we're in the middle of dinner. Would you mind waiting for him?"

"I wouldn't mind, no. But I'd prefer to come and sit at the table with you. What are you serving, by the way? I hope you don't mind my asking. You see, I was in the middle of dinner myself."

"Avocado and grapefruit salad and seafood Newburg."

"Sounds great. Did you make the seafood yourself?"

"We have a cook."

"Congratulations. Good cooks are hard to find these days."

"I didn't say she was a good cook. . . . Are you by any chance inviting yourself for dinner?"

"The thought crossed my mind."

"This is—this is really extraordinary."

"I don't agree. Put a hungry man on the trail of seafood Newburg and what he does is quite ordinary."

"I don't know what Mr. Aragon will say when he gets here if you're sitting having dinner with us."

"Aragon? Now, he's pretty small potatoes for a big man like your husband. Potatoes. There goes my mind again, back to food."

"I've never been in a situation like this before in my life."

"As a matter of fact, neither have I. But we mustn't shut ourselves off from new experiences, must we?"

"Come this way."

It wasn't the most gracious invitation he'd ever received but it was the only one for dinner that night, so he followed her down the hall.

Jasper was standing at the head of the dining room table, his left hand in his pocket.

"Hilton, this is Lieutenant Peterson," Frieda said. "He has kindly consented to join us for dinner."

The lieutenant nodded. "Glad to meet you, Mr. Jasper. I don't imagine the feeling is mutual."

"No, it's not."

"Ah well, suppose we forget business for a while and act like new friends about to break bread together for the first time."

Jasper's only reply was to pull out a chair and then put his own plate of salad, which he hadn't touched, in front of the lieutenant. Frieda turned up the heat under the silver chafing dish that contained the seafood.

She said, "My husband and I aren't having wine with dinner tonight but I'll open a bottle for you if you like."

"Not while I'm on duty."

The lieutenant ate quickly and quietly with only an occasional remark about the weather, the food, the state of the nation. Neither of the Jaspers made any attempt to converse. Frieda served the food and Jasper pushed it around on his plate in a pretense of eating.

Afterward, the lieutenant said, "Excellent, excellent. I truly appreciate having a home-cooked meal now and then. Since my wife died I've probably eaten more Big Macs and fries than any man in town."

Jasper took a deep breath and held it for a moment before speaking. "Why are you here, Lieutenant?"

"As I told your wife, the desk sergeant received a phone call about six-thirty. He played the tape of it for me. It was the voice of a young woman, a girl probably, who'd been listening to the six o'clock news and heard about Roger Lennard's death. A man named Abercrombie had spoken rather freely to the press describing someone who'd visited Lennard in the late morning. She claimed the description fitted you."

"I see."

"A lot of policemen would like people to believe that we go around solving crimes by taking fingerprints and making plaster casts and ballistics tests. Now these things all look good in a courtroom once the criminal is on trial. But how he's caught is usually a different story. Somebody squealed, a disgruntled employee or partner, a jealous lover, a cast-off wife. These are the people who solve crimes. If it weren't for the young woman's phone call I wouldn't be here. Tall man in a gray suit and Panama hat —that's not much to go on. Add a name and address, and the picture changes. Did you go to see Roger Lennard this morning?"

"I'd like to hear that tape."

"That's not an answer to my question, Mr. Jasper."

"I'll answer your questions if you let me listen to the tape."

"No," Frieda said. "No, you won't. You're not to say anything until Mr. Aragon—"

"Be quiet, Frieda. . . . What about it, Lieutenant? Do we have a deal?"

"Sounds fair to me."

"I want to hear the tape first."

"Now that part isn't so fair," the lieutenant said. "Maybe you think you might recognize the voice?"

"I might."

"We'll have to go out to my car. I brought the tape with me. I intended to play it for you anyway."

Frieda made one more attempt to stop him but he pushed her aside. "Let me handle my own affairs," he said. "I'm a big boy now."

"You don't eat like one. You're a stupid, pigheaded little boy."

"I hate to break up a good old-fashioned family row," the lieutenant said. "But sometimes I have to. Let's go, Mr. Jasper. Would you like to come along too, Mrs. Jasper? It's the least I can do in return for the excellent meal."

"I hope you get indigestion," Frieda said.

The tape was brief:

"Police Department, Sergeant Kowalski speaking."

"Hello. Is this the right place to phone to tell you something?"

"Yes ma'm, if you're got something to tell."

"I heard it on the radio about Roger Lennard being dead. Is it true? I guess it must be true or they wouldn't say it to everybody like that."

"Yes ma'm."

"They said a man quarreled with Roger. I know who it was. He's mean, he's a mean old man."

"Just a minute and I'll transfer this—"

"His name is Hilton Jasper and he lives at twelve hundred Via Vista."

"Would you give me your name please, ma'm?"

The tape ended with a click. The voice was Cleo's.

The lieutenant said, "Think that might be someone you know, Mr. Jasper?"

"No."

"Maybe you'd care to hear it again?"

"No, thanks," Jasper said. "I had an idea it might be a secretary I had to fire last week."

"Disgruntled employee, right?"

"Yes."

"I didn't think a man in your position had much to do with the hiring and firing of secretaries."

"There are exceptions."

"I'm sure there are. Let's play it again to make sure it wasn't your disgruntled employee, shall we?"

"No. *No.*"

"Usually when we're having somebody try to identify a voice, we play the tape several times."

"There's no need for that. It wasn't my former secretary."

"I know that, Mr. Jasper. Who was it?"

Jasper shook his head.

"You won't identify the caller?"

"I can't."

"Can't, won't, same difference as far as I'm concerned. I don't get an answer. . . . It sounded like a girl to me. Would you agree with that?"

"I guess so."

"Perhaps it was one of those girls at the special school where Roger Lennard worked."

"Perhaps."

"Well, you've heard the tape. Now I'd like to hear your answers to a few questions. Shall we go back into the house?"

"I'd prefer to stay here."

"Mrs. Jasper?"

"Mrs. Jasper."

"Feisty woman. I like the type but they're tough to live with. Any kids?"

"We have a son, Edward. He'll be a senior at Cal Poly this fall."

"No daughters?"

"No."

"Once in a while our crimes are solved for us by disgruntled daughters as well as employees. . . . How long have you known Lennard?"

"Not long."

"What made you decide to call on him this morning?"

"I prefer not to answer that."

"Your prefers and my prefers aren't going to jibe, are they?"

"I'll make a simple statement about my actions this morning without going into motives. I quarreled with Lennard, I hit him twice, he didn't fall down, I left. Those are the facts. I can't tell you any more at this time."

"You haven't told me anything I didn't know."

"I confessed to hitting him. That will have to be enough for now."

The lieutenant rewound the tape and played it through again. "You'll notice, Mr. Jasper, that the girl refers to Mr. Lennard as Roger."

"Yes, I noticed."

"She was evidently a friend of his."

"Yes."

"And you evidently were not a friend either of his or of hers. She called you a mean old man."

"So I heard."

"How old are you?"

"Forty-four."

"That's not old," the lieutenant said. "Is her other claim also exaggerated?"

"Am I mean? Apparently someone thinks so."

"Some secret enemy?"

"You might say that."

"Oh, no, I wouldn't say that at all, Mr. Jasper. I'm convinced you know this girl, perhaps very well. Have you been fooling around?"

"No."

"I believe you. She didn't sound like the kind of person who'd appeal to a man of your social status. She's definitely lower class, don't you agree?"

"I'm not in the habit of judging a person's social position by listening to a few sentences on tape," Jasper said stiffly. "Now if you'll excuse me, I'll—"

"Who was the girl, Jasper?"

"I can't say."

"Okay. That's all for now. You're free to go back in the house, watch TV or go to bed, or finish the argument with your wife, whatever."

"Aren't you going to wait for Aragon?"

"Why should I?" the lieutenant said. "I'd probably get even less information with him around. . . . Thank your wife again for the dinner. And tell her I never get indigestion from food, only from people."

The lieutenant returned to headquarters. Kowalski, the desk sergeant who'd played him the tape on the radiophone, was still on duty. He was eating a ham sandwich that oozed the bilious yellow of mustard. A young woman in uniform was sitting at a desk with a typewriter in front of her, scratching her head with a pencil. Nothing much seemed to be happening, except possibly inside the young woman's head.

"Quiet night," Kowalski said. "Anything we can do for you, lieutenant?"

"I'd like to see the city directory."

"Sarah will get it for you. Hey, Sarah."

The young woman dropped her pencil. "Don't you hey-Sarah me or I'll report you to the National Organization for Women."

"You reported me twice this month."

"Three times and out."

"All right, all right. Sarah, honorable policeperson, would you please drag your beautiful butt over to the shelf and get the lieutenant the city directory?"

"That 'beautiful butt' remark could be construed as sexual harassment."

"Get the directory, kiddo," the lieutenant said.

He took the directory back to his office, a small room, hardly more than a cubicle, sparsely furnished with two straight-backed chairs in addition to the swivel chair behind his desk. There was also a filing cabinet, and a water cooler used mainly to water the Boston fern on a five-foot stand in the corner, its fronds reaching all the way to the floor. Except for the standard electronic equipment, the desk was almost bare: no heavy paperweight that could be used as a weapon and no papers that could be spied on. On one side there was a small graceful porpoise carved out of ironwood and on the other a photograph of three people in tennis clothes: a fair-haired woman and two teen-aged boys.

The house at 1200 Via Vista was listed in the directory as jointly owned by Frieda and Hilton Jasper, with Edward Jasper, Cleo Jasper, Paolo Trocadero and Valencia Ybarra as residents. Trocadero and Ybarra were probably servants and Jasper had mentioned his son Edward, but claimed to have no daughters. So who was Cleo and why hadn't her name come up in the conversation?

He called the record room and asked for any recent information on Hilton or Cleo Jasper. Ten minutes later Sarah appeared with a card bearing the name Hilton Jasper, the time of his arrival at the police station, the nature of his complaint, a missing person described as his sister, Cleo, a student at Holbrook Hall. Attached to the card was a passport-size picture of an unsmiling pretty girl with long straight hair. The absence of any further information indicated that no action had been taken on the case.

The lieutenant leaned back in his chair, his hands clasped behind his head. His eyes moved back and forth as if he were watching a computer readout on the ceiling.

Cleo Jasper. Runaway. Student at Holbrook Hall. Victim of some degree of mental or emotional impairment. Member of a wealthy family. Alive as of six-thirty. Still in town, since a nonlocal radio station wouldn't bother to report the death of someone as unimportant as Lennard.

No indication even of Cleo's existence had been given by the Jaspers, Mrs. Holbrook, or Aragon. What were they protecting—the girl's future? Their own pride? The reputation of the school?

The lieutenant yawned, stretched, studied the picture on the card again.

"Cleo," he said aloud. "Where the hell are you?"

12

The mail was delivered to Holbrook Hall the following morning at ten o'clock. Rachel Holbrook had been waiting for it, pacing around her office as if she were measuring its precincts, glancing at her wristwatch every few minutes. When she saw the truck coming up the driveway she went to meet the postman at the front door.

He was a plump, cheerful young man who felt it was part of his job to give his important customers a preview of the day's haul.

"Lots of throwaway stuff this morning, Mrs. Holbrook. And bills—I guess you can't run a place like this without a bunch of bills."

"Thank you, Harry, I'll just take it and—"

"New issues of *Reader's Digest*, *Psychology Today*, *AudioVisual Journal*. Letters for the kids, naturally. I always wondered, do they read their own letters or are they read to them?

"A catalogue of playground equipment. I'd like to borrow that when you've finished, if you don't mind, Mrs. Holbrook. My kids are getting old enough now to use things like that in the yard."

"I'll save it for you, Harry. Goodbye."

The box of mail was so heavy she could hardly carry it back to her office. The job of separating it was usually left to her secretary but this morning she did it herself. She found the letter from Roger Lennard almost immediately. It looked like any other letter, but it was the first she'd ever received from a dead man and it seemed to give off a faintly sour odor.

She called Aragon at his apartment.

"Roger's letter has arrived," she said. "I think you should be here when I open it."

"Why?"

"I'm beginning to wonder if I did the correct thing. Yesterday it seemed so logical and right. Now I don't know. I'm frightened."

He hesitated. Then: "I should be there in about twenty minutes. Take it easy."

"Roger meant me to have it. It's not as though I took something that didn't belong to me, do you think?"

"I think you should stop second-guessing until I get there."

He came within twenty minutes.

It was a cool morning, with the sun just starting to break through the low overcast of clouds. Along the driveway up to the school there were patches of moisture under the big trees where the night fog had condensed and dripped from the leaves, the gray lace of the acacias, the leathery loquats, the prickly oaks and feathery pepper trees. It would be another three months before the rains started, and these night fogs were what kept the trees alive.

Rachel Holbrook was standing on the front steps talking

to two girl students. When she saw Aragon she dismissed the girls with a smile and a gesture. They walked away, giggling, whispering behind their hands, glancing back at the new arrival.

"Good morning, Mr. Aragon," she said formally and loud enough for the girls to overhear. "You've come about the accounting, of course."

"Yes. It's a good morning for accounting."

"Come in." She added, after she closed the door, "The whole school knows something is up. I don't want to add any fuel to the fire."

The drapes in her office were closed. Light came from the fluorescent fixtures in the ceiling and the draftsman's lamp on her desk, angled to shine directly on the letter from Roger Lennard. The setting looked a little too theatrical. Aragon was not sure what role he was expected to play in the production.

She handed him the letter and told him to open it.

"Why me?" he said.

"It will prove that I haven't already done so, for one thing."

"And for another?"

She didn't answer directly. "I've had a chance to appraise the situation and I realize now that I might have done something quite criminal."

"There's no such thing as quite criminal, Mrs. Holbrook. It is or it isn't."

"Very well. I removed evidence from the scene of a possible crime. But you will be my witness to the fact that I didn't know what was in here and my motive in taking it was solely to spare Roger in case he survived."

"That sounds very noble. But I don't think Lieutenant Peterson is much of a believer in nobility."

"Are you?"

"Sometimes." This wasn't one of the times. He had

driven to L.A. the previous night on business for Smedler and hadn't arrived home until three o'clock in the morning. He felt tired and hungry and irritable.

"I don't claim that my motives were noble, Mr. Aragon. They were human, that's all."

"It's your letter, Mrs. Holbrook. You open it."

She slit the envelope with her thumbnail and shook the contents out on her desk. There were almost a dozen sheets of paper. Some appeared to be completed letters, some were half-finished and some sheets bore only a few words. One of the completed letters began *Dear Mrs. Holbrook.* She read it aloud in a low, cautious voice.

"Dear Mrs. Holbrook:

You have been more like a mother to me than my own mother. You have respected my work, which is all I'm good for, maybe not even that any more. You have encouraged me and given me your friendship.

I am writing this to say goodbye and to thank you for your kindness and generosity. I know you will not judge this as an act of cowardice on my part. It is, quite simply, inevitable, something I have been considering for a long time.

Last year when I was excommunicated from the church you took me in and gave me back some of my self-confidence.

Since I have been a practicing homosexual I will not be able to join my family in the afterworld. I can only hope that there is another place, perhaps a better place, where I can be with truly good people like you. I go to my death believing there must be such a place.

I have been writing off and on all morning and now I don't know what to do with the stuff. I just don't think people will want to read what I have to say. I am putting it all into this envelope and you can do with it whatever you think best. I've always trusted your judgment.

148

Please remember me as someone who has felt blessed by your friendship.

Roger"

Mrs. Holbrook got up and walked to the window as though she were about to look out through the closed drapes. She made no sound, but Aragon knew she was weeping.

"I'm sorry," he said. "I'll read the rest if you like."

She nodded and he sat down at her desk and picked up one of the other sheets of paper.

"To Whom It May Concern If Anybody:

I tried, I really tried. I prayed to God but he turned out to be a cruel old man in the sky who knows more about hate than about love. I tried, everyone laughed but I tried. And failed. Failed failed failed. Let that be my epitaph, Roger Lennard, he tried, he failed.

What message do I want to leave to the world? A curse on all pious bigots everywhere."

Another letter was to his parents.

"Dear Mom and Dad:

It was good to hear your voices on the phone the other night. You sounded so happy, Mom, when I told you the news about my getting married. And I was happy too. I really thought it would work out. Cleo admires me and respects me.

I can almost hear you saying, the girl must be crazy. Well, she is, sort of. But she wants to have a family and so do I. I've always loved kids. My head was filled with hope. But all the time I had this terrible turmoil inside me, despair, hate, rage. It is impossible for me to make a family, impossible. Oh, how I can picture Dad scowling over that because he thinks that men are first and foremost created to make families. But what if they can't? Can't can't can't what if they can't?"

Another unfinished letter was addressed to Cleo.

"Dear little Cleo, you should never have come to me with your troubles. I often told you at school that you could, but when you did, when you suddenly appeared out of the blue, I got carried away. I forgot I was supposed to be objective. I thought, why not? Why can't Cleo and I have children like normal people? All of a sudden I had real hope for the future. I would change, you would change, we would change each other. We would have a family, I could be a good Mormon again.

I liked the feel of you in my arms. Your skin was so soft you seemed made of silk and flowers. Then you began to talk about Ted. Ted did this, Ted did that. You never meant to tease me, you had no idea how much I was suffering. Then you said, Oh Roger, are you one of those funny people? And I said yes. Yes, I'm one of the funnies, funny ha ha, funny peculiar, funny split your sides. I'm one of the funnies, so please laugh, Cleo, don't lie there like a stone flower.

I have written a poem about us, Cleo.

> Funny sky
> Funny sea,
> Funny I,
> Funny me.
> Funny me
> Funny us,
> Funnily
> Oblivious.

Oblivious. I like that word. It sounds like a nice place to go.

Forgive me, Cleo, if I have harmed you in any way, if I have given you ideas beyond your grasp. You were so anxious to become what you called a real person. And I was so anxious to help you become one. We had high hopes and high failures. This is how the world ends."

Some of the other sheets of paper contained only a few words.

"Cruel. All around me is cruel. I am afraid. Nightmare, daymare, morningmare, afternoonmare. What is it all about? It is too late. It is too late for anyone to tell me."

"Tim, Tim my beloved, please forgive me. I had to choose between you and the church. What else could I do, what other decision could I make with the family on my back like that? Please, Tim. Please don't judge me harshly."

"To the Probate Court:

I, Roger Lennard, mens sana in corpore sano, would like my worldly possessions distributed as follows:
My books to Holbrook Hall
My classical records to the Public Library.
All other possessions to my dear friend, Timothy North.

Roger Lennard"

"Mom, Mom I can't stand never seeing you again"

Slowly and carefully Aragon put the papers back in the envelope.
"I'm sorry," he said again.
"Yes."
"Lieutenant Peterson will have to be informed of this right away. What are you going to tell him?"

"That it came in the mail."

"That's all?"

"That's all."

"He won't be satisfied," Aragon said. "He'll want to know, for instance, if this is the same envelope you were seen posting yesterday."

"On the other hand," she said, "he might be so happy at having Roger's death proved a suicide that he'll let the matter drop."

"I don't think the lieutenant will ever be that happy."

"We'll have to wait and see."

She unlocked the drawer where she kept her personal belongings during office hours and placed the envelope in her purse. "I suppose I should deliver it to him myself."

"Yes."

"It would be kind of you to come along for moral support."

"Better if I don't," Aragon said. "Lawyers aren't very high on the lieutenant's popularity poll."

The red light on the intercom had started to blink and Mrs. Holbrook switched on the speaker. "Yes, Richie?"

"The captain is here to see you, Mrs. Holbrook."

"But I didn't— I wasn't exp— Wait a minute." She turned to Aragon. "Captain? Isn't that a higher rank than lieutenant?"

"Yes."

"Please wait. I'm not sure how to handle this. The entire school will be aroused if he arrived here in a police car."

But he hadn't come in a police car. The captain's hat he wore could have been purchased in any maritime shop along the coast, and his well-tailored navy-blue blazer and white slacks weren't the kind of clothing found in a policeman's locker.

The man was about fifty, with a round red face and bushy sun-bleached eyebrows that seemed to have a life of their own, like blond caterpillars. He gave off an odor of cologne and bourbon and cigar smoke.

"Well, well, what's going on here?" he said jovially. "A séance?"

"You might call it that," Mrs. Holbrook replied.

"Include me in. I've never been to a séance. But first let's get a little light in here." He went over to the windows and began pulling open the drapes. "If I'm going to see ghosts I want the genuine article that'll stand up to daylight."

"Mr. Whitfield, this is Mr. Aragon."

Whitfield's handshake was firm and hearty. "I was in a town in Spain once called Aragon. Not much of a place but it had some pretty girls. You couldn't get near them, though. There were a dozen old crones surrounding each one."

Aragon couldn't think of a suitable comment, so he kept quiet.

"I have nothing against Spain," Whitfield added. "The fact is, I'm not at home on land. Any land, anywhere. The sea's where I live. I'm heading for Ensenada tomorrow. One of my crewmen wants to check on his wife and I figure, why not? Some of the *muchachas* in these Mexican ports can be pretty lively."

Failing for the second time to get a response from Aragon, he turned his attention to Mrs. Holbrook. "I came as soon as I got your message."

Mrs. Holbrook looked surprised. She had been trying to contact him for two days but she had left no message and no name. "I don't quite understand, Mr. Whitfield."

"The girl in your office caught me as I was leaving my condo. In fact, the phone rang as I was going out the door.

She told me to come to the school to discuss Donny's curriculum. She didn't sound too sure of the word *curriculum*. Maybe you'd better tell her what it means."

"When a call is made from this office concerning a student I handle it personally or through my secretary. His name is Richard. I have no female employees authorized to perform such duties, and if I had she would certainly be familiar with words like curriculum."

"What's going on around here? I tell you, I had this phone call from some girl at the school and she said I was to come right over and discuss Donny's curriculum. Hell, it was that word that brought me over here so fast. I thought maybe the kid was finally straightening out. Any other time I've heard from the school it's been about one of Donny's famous emergencies, like when he stole the laundry truck and rammed it into a tree."

Aragon spoke for the first time since Whitfield's arrival. "What else did the girl say, Mr. Whitfield?"

"Nothing much. She emphasized that I was to come here immediately. I failed to understand the reason for the big hurry but I went along with the request. So here I am—at considerable loss of time, if I may add—and no one's even expecting me."

"Did she give a name?"

"No."

"Do you remember her exact words?"

"Well, she just said, 'this is Mrs. Holbrook's office at Holbrook Hall.' No, wait a minute. She sort of slurred the name of the school. It almost sounded like Holy Hall."

"The students often call it that," Mrs. Holbrook said.

"So it was one of those damn little half-wits playing a joke on me. That's the thanks I get for practically supporting this so-called school."

"It is more than so-called, Mr. Whitfield. It's a real

154

school which takes students the other schools don't want, can't manage, can't teach."

"Hell, I don't want Donny to learn Latin and a lot of crap like that. I just want him to learn to behave himself, keep his nose clean."

"We don't guarantee results. And we don't teach Latin. We try to teach acceptable social behavior such as the avoidance of profanity."

"Well, goddam it, I'm sorry. But the trouble I've had with that kid—"

"You're going to have more, Mr. Whitfield."

"What does that mean?"

"We'd better sit down and discuss it." To Aragon she said, "I was about to deliver this envelope. I wonder if you'd be so kind as to do it for me. It's a rush job and I may be occupied here for some time."

Aragon had no choice. He took the envelope and departed. There was no exchange of goodbyes.

As he was walking toward the parking lot he looked back and saw Whitfield through the window, slumped in one of the leather chairs. His right leg was slung over the arm of the chair and his chin was resting on his fist. Upside down on the desk was his captain's hat, a symbol of his store-bought authority.

Aragon left the envelope at Police Headquarters and drove down to the harbor. The harbormaster's office was on the second floor of a small building beside the yacht club. From it the entire coastline could be seen for miles in either direction, as well as everything that was happening on the breakwater and the wharf and at the marina. The entrance to the harbor lay between the end of the wharf and the breakwater. Almost every day its depth varied according to the movement of sand by the tides and currents. In spite of almost continual dredging, the channel was sometimes blocked entirely for the larger craft. On many occasions the commercial fishing fleet had to wait at anchor outside the harbor while the other half was trapped inside like grounded whales.

Today the entrance was navigable. A ketch, still under power, was heading for the open sea, raising its mainsail. A boat that serviced the oil platforms was picking up speed as it left the five-mile-an-hour limit of the harbor.

The harbormaster, Sprague, an ex-Seabee, had had an indoor job for half a dozen years but it was too late to prevent the sun damage that mottled his face in the form of skin cancers. Now in his sixties, he had difficulty remembering names and faces but he never forgot a boat and he considered all the craft tied up in the harbor as his personal fleet. Only God and the weather outranked him.

He was on the phone when Aragon entered.

"Hold it, Wavewalker. I've had two more complaints against you for littering."

"Hell, a few beer cans ain't littering. They sink to the bottom."

"Sure, and pretty soon you'll be trying to float on a pile of rust. So clean up your act. Where are you heading?"

"*The Ruby*. She's laying in her usual supply of caviar and Chivas Regal."

"When will you be back?"

"As soon as possible. You think we like rolling around on this tub?"

"Get a horse."

Sprague motioned Aragon to sit down. "What's on your mind?"

Aragon offered one of his business cards. Sprague studied it for a moment, then dropped it on his desk.

"I'm interested in Peter Whitfield's yacht," Aragon said.

"Interested in what way?"

"I hear it's heading for Ensenada tomorrow."

Sprague raised his binoculars. They were very powerful and heavy and his hands shook as he adjusted the focus. When they steadied he said, "It looks as if they're getting ready for something. They've taken off the sail covers."

"May I see?"

"Go ahead. It's the blue ketch *Spindrift*, Marina J, port-side."

Aragon took the binoculars. He had more trouble steadying them than Sprague had had, but eventually he could make out the large boat that bore the name *Spindrift*. Two men were on deck, dressed like twins in dark-blue pants and blue-and-white diagonally striped T-shirts. One was folding the dark-blue covers that protected the sails from the weather; the other was sitting astride the boom.

He said, "What's the little flag at the top of the mast?"

"That's the burgee indicating the captain's on board."

"Who is the captain?"

"Whitfield likes to take the wheel but he doesn't have his captain's papers. The boat's actually run by Manny Ocho and a couple of permanent crewmen. Whitfield calls himself captain. A lot of people do who hang around here. It's a case of more captains than boats."

"Would the burgee be flying if Ocho was on board without Whitfield?"

"No, no. Whitfield couldn't allow that."

"Can you get me in touch with the boat?"

"No problem."

There was some delay in getting through to the *Spindrift*, then a man's voice answered, "Yes."

"Hi, Manny. What's up?"

"Oh, Mr. Sprague. We pretty soon get under way."

"No goodbyes, no farewell party?"

"Not this time, no sir."

"Is the captain on board?"

"No. Wait—wait a minute—"

Another man's voice came on the line. "You're damn tootin' the captain's on board. Who wants to know?"

"Sprague. I'm just checking."

"Yeah? Well, everything's A-OK, Sprague, old boy. We're off and running."

"Where to?"

"The moon, man, the moon."

"Hold it, please." Sprague put his hand over the mouthpiece and said to Aragon, "You want to talk to Whitfield? He sounds drunk."

"I saw Whitfield less than half an hour ago and he wasn't drunk," Aragon said. "I'd better go out there and check things out."

"Sure. I'd go with you but I can't leave my post. Take the ramp nearest the breakwater. The gate's open. These guys are always squawking about security but they leave the gates open for convenience."

"Thanks, Mr. Sprague."

"Sure. Tell Manny, next time I want a party."

Some of the boats were owned by people who lived out of town. These seldom left the harbor. Others were used only on weekends and for the sailing races on Wet Wednesdays. A few were permanent residences, as permanent as the city's bylaws allowed. A Monterey seiner was coming in loaded with fish, moving low and slow in the water, surrounded by a noisy tangle of gulls.

A lone pelican, sitting aloof and self-sufficient on the breakwater railing, viewed these barbarous antics with contempt. He didn't need handouts, though he was not above accepting offerings from the fishermen who lined the breakwater. A pelican had occupied that same spot for years. Aragon and his school friends used to come down to the harbor on Saturdays and fish solely in order to feed the bird, flattered by its friendship. Perhaps it was the same pelican, or a son or grandson.

There wasn't enough activity in Marina J for Aragon's approach to go unnoticed. When he reached the *Spindrift* there was nobody on deck. The boat seemed suddenly deserted, though a radio was playing rock music in one of the cabins.

He called out, "Whitfield?"

He knew there were at least four people on board—Manny Ocho, the two crewmen and the man who had claimed to be Captain Whitfield—but none of them responded to his call. There was further evidence that the *Spindrift* wasn't expecting visitors. The gangplank had been drawn up. When he'd first seen the ketch from the harbormaster's office the gangplank had been down like a welcome mat.

"Captain Whitfield?"

There was a slight response this time. Someone turned off the radio. A dark-winged gull perched on the bowsprit let out a raucous laugh, then went back to his task of cleaning the oil off his breast feathers.

"Manny Ocho?" Aragon switched to Spanish. "What's going on down there? Are you in trouble?"

Ocho started to reply but someone yelled, "Speak English, you bastard."

"*Ching tu madre,*" Ocho said.

"I told you, speak English." The voice rose hysterically. "What's that mean, that *chinga* business?"

"Guess."

"I am guessing, you bad-mouthed little creep. I ought to kill you."

"You need me, I not need you."

Aragon was forgotten for the moment as the argument continued. Only a couple of feet of water separated the ramp from the deck of the *Spindrift*. He jumped it easily and landed on the deck. The door was closed to the forward cabin where the argument was taking place. Aragon pounded on it with his fist and there was immediate silence. Then the door was jerked open so violently that he almost fell down the steps into the cabin. After the glare of the sun it was dark and he could see very little at first. But the voice was recognizable, half whine, half bluster:

"Well, well, look who's dropped in, my old pal that leaves his car keys in the ignition."

3

MERMAID

13

When Cleo woke up, the boat was rocking slightly with the rising tide. She wasn't ready to wake up yet, so she kept her eyes closed and rolled her head back and forth on the pillow and thought of the baby inside her rolling back and forth too, rocking, rocking, rock-a-bye baby. She held another pillow clasped tight against her belly. This second one was made of foam rubber and it felt smooth and yielding like flesh. Sometimes, in a foggy moment, she believed it was real flesh, her own real baby. But usually she knew it wasn't, that her real baby was deep down inside her, very tiny, hardly bigger than a grain of sugar.

Once she tied the pillow around her waist inside her dress and went downtown, walking along the streets and into the stores. People looked at her oddly.

Some were pitying: "Why, you poor child, you're scarcely more than a child yourself. How far gone are you?"

"Quite," Cleo said solemnly. "Quite far gone."

Some were contemptuous. "Don't they teach about contraceptives in school? Look at her. Probably on welfare.

That brat of hers will probably be on welfare too. And *we'll* be picking up the bills."

One woman reached out and touched Cleo on the stomach.

Cleo drew back, surprised and frightened. "What did you do that for?"

"For luck. Didn't you ever hear that?"

"No."

"Whenever you see a woman big with child you touch her on the stomach for luck."

She went back to the motel near the beach and told Roger about the woman who touched the baby for luck, only it wasn't the baby.

"Why did you do a thing like that?" he said, turning red with anger. "People will think you're crazy."

"But there really is a baby deep inside. And you're going to be the father and I'm going to be the mother. You promised, Roger. That very first day when I came to you and told you what happened with Ted and me, you said you would take care of me. You said you would see to it that Hilton wouldn't take the baby away and have me fixed like he did our cat. You promised, Roger."

"Yes."

"And after this one, we'll have some more. Boy, girl, boy, girl, or two boys and two girls, whichever you think is best. It wouldn't be fair to have just one child. It would always be lonely, the way I am."

"What if we can't make it, Cleo, if things don't work out?"

"You're always telling me that people can work anything out if they really try, that people can *make* things work out. You told me that."

"Yes."

"You weren't lying?"

"I didn't intend to lie, Cleo. Perhaps I only spoke too soon, too optimistically."

She began to cry then, and Roger held her in his arms, trying to soothe her, stroking her hair, brushing her tears away with his mouth.

"Come inside, Roger," she said. "Come in and visit our baby. Come inside."

"Not now."

"Why not?"

"The dog," he said. "The dog wants out. I have to go and walk him."

"Oh, I'm sick of that dog. He's always interfering like this. He's not my friend anymore. . . . Will you come back soon?"

"Yes."

Roger was gone a long time. When he came back he told her he'd arranged to have the dog returned to the Jaspers. He was very pale and smelled of liquor.

"Are you going to visit the baby now, Roger?"

"I want to."

They lay down again and she clasped her legs around his and held him tight against her. She could feel him struggling to get away and pretty soon he began to cry.

"God forgive me. I'm sorry, Cleo. Sorry, sorry, sorry."

Roger always said things three times when he really meant them, so that was the night she found out that things sometimes didn't work out no matter how hard people tried.

This time when Roger left he took his clothes with him and that was the end of the marriage.

She phoned Ted at the house the next morning and told him a sort of lie. She said Hilton had kicked her out just the way he had kicked Ted out and she was staying at a motel because she had nowhere to go. She asked him to help her find a place to live. He said he'd be right down, though he sounded rather peculiar.

She waited for him outside the motel.

His first words were, "That story you gave me on the phone was a lot of bull, wasn't it?"

"A little," she said. "Not a whole lot."

"So what actually happened?"

"I ran away. I ran away because they kicked you out and I didn't think it was fair."

"Why'd you do that?"

"Because I like you."

"Oh, come off it, kid." But he sounded flattered. "You shouldn't have run away. You know you can't look after yourself. What do you intend to do?"

"I was going to get married."

"What changed your mind?"

"I found out he was already married."

"Hang in there. He might divorce her."

"It's not a her."

"So why did you drag me into this?"

"I don't know."

She did know, though she hadn't known for long. When she telephoned him for help she had only a vague idea in her mind, but now she was perfectly sure. Ted had nice features, he laughed easily, he played games well, he surfed and skied, and he could teach all these things to a son the way a good father should.

They walked along the waterfront. Ted told her his mother had given him enough money to live on for the summer, and that if his father hadn't relented by next fall she intended to sell some bonds to finance his senior year in college. Cleo asked him where he was going for the summer. He wasn't certain.

"Aspen, maybe," he said. "It's not as lively as it is in the winter but there's still plenty of action if you look for it."

"I was in Catalina once." She recalled the trip vividly because it had been the only real experience in her life, with no Hilton or Frieda around, no Mrs. Holbrook or counselors, just the waves and the sea birds and a pleasant little man who ran the boat. She even remembered his name, Manny Ocho, because there weren't many names in her life to remember. She saw the little man once in a while because on her free afternoons she sometimes took a bus down to the harbor and looked for the boat. If it was there she waved to the skipper or whoever was on board. But usually it was gone and the space where it was supposed to be was empty. She felt left out, like a little girl not invited to a party.

She said, "Do you think I'd like Aspen?"

"Sure. Why not?"

"I've got a thousand dollars."

Ted laughed. "That's about four days' worth in Aspen."

This was a shock. She thought a person could live for a whole year on a thousand dollars. "Where is Aspen?"

"In the mountains in Colorado."

"Is it healthful?"

"In some ways, I guess. In others, no."

"I mean, does it have a healthful climate? I need a healthful climate."

"Look, kid, the most healthful climate for you is right here. You'd better call my parents and tell them you'll be home pretty soon. Will you do that?"

"If you want me to, Ted."

"Listen, what I want has nothing to do with anything. It's simple logic. You know what logic is, common sense."

"If you're driving alone some place and I wanted to go to the very same place, wouldn't it be common sense to take me along?"

"No," he said. "No, no."

"Why do men always say things three times? Why not two or four?"

"Okay, we'll make it four. *No.*"

"I didn't really ask anyway. I just said, wouldn't it be common sense?"

"Listen, you wanted me to help you find an apartment or someplace to live. I can drive you around and we'll look for vacancy signs. And that'll be the end of it. Understand?"

"Yes."

"You're sure?"

"Yes. But let's keep walking. It's such a neat day and you and I haven't ever really talked before."

"All right. We'll walk and talk. But don't start getting any funny ideas. You and I are going our separate ways."

She gazed up at him wistfully. "But Aspen sounds so pretty."

"It's not that pretty. Besides, I may not go there. It's the first name that occurred to me, is all. I may go to Borneo."

"I never heard of Borneo. Does it have a healthful climate?"

"Jeez," Ted said. "Let's walk."

"But does it have a healthful climate?"

"It's a jungle infested with giant snakes and rodents."

"Then why are you going there?"

"To get away from people who ask dumb questions."

"I have to ask dumb questions," she said. "I'm dumb, aren't I?"

"Come on, come on, come on."

She didn't move.

"Now what's the matter?"

"You did it again, Ted."

"Did what?"

168

"Said something three times, instead of two or four."

Ted said, "Move it, kid," and gave her a little push. They began walking out toward the breakwater, past the Coast Guard headquarters, the marine accessories store and yacht brokers' offices, a fish market, and finally the breakwater itself. The tide was low and a small group of children were picking up mussels off the rocks on the sea side. On the other side, between two rows of marinas, a western grebe was diving for dinner. It came up with a fish in its beak and maneuvered it around until the fish could be swallowed head first. The bird's long thin neck bulged for a moment or two. Cleo didn't like to see creatures eating other creatures, so she closed her eyes and clung to Ted's arm to help keep her balance.

When she opened her eyes again, there was the *Spindrift*, sky-blue and white, with dark-blue sail covers. At first she thought there was no one on deck; then she saw Manny Ocho about three quarters of the way up the mainmast, inspecting some rigging.

She called to him and waved. "Manny, it's me, Cleo."

He waved back. "Hey, Cleo, why you not in school?"

"I'm on vacation."

"Pretty soon, I'm on vacation too."

"Where are you going?"

"Ensenada, see my wife and kids, make sure everything's okey doke. Who's your friend?"

"Ted."

"Want to come aboard?"

"Oh, yes, I'd love to."

"Better go the long way round. Too far to jump, too dirty to swim."

They walked back to the entrance ramp of the marina, with Cleo pulling Ted by the hand to hurry him along.

"Who the hell wants to go on a boat?" he said. "I

thought I was supposed to help you find an apartment."

"That can wait. I still have the room at the motel where Roger and I were going to spend our honeymoon."

"Has it occurred to you that I might have affairs of my own to settle?"

"Oh, Ted, you don't really want to go to Borneo, do you? Maybe Manny might let us ride along with him to Ensenada. Wouldn't that be fun?"

"I doubt it."

"I bet it's a lot nicer than Borneo," Cleo said. "I bet it's not infected with snakes."

When they reached the *Spindrift* the gangplank was down, and they went on board as Manny Ocho slid down from the mast on a rope like a circus performer.

"I show off," he said, examining the palms of his hands. "Hurts like hell. Cleo, you looking good, happy. This your young man?"

"She's my aunt," Ted said.

"Your aunt, ho ho. A joke, no?"

"It's no joke."

"You're a big boy to have such a cute little aunt. Me, I got nine, ten aunts, all old and fat and ugly."

Cleo giggled, hiding her face against Ted's sleeve. He didn't seem to mind. She really was cute.

Manny showed them around the *Spindrift* with great pride. In a sense it belonged more to him than to Whitfield, who merely held the owner's papers and couldn't have taken the boat out of the harbor by himself.

The captain's quarters occupied the entire forward cabin. It was spacious and luxuriously furnished, but its teak paneling was marred by Whitfield's collection of pinups, some of them signed, and its thick, red wool carpeting bore the stains of too many spilled drinks. A television set that projected its picture on a large screen was turned on to a baseball game, and a crewman was sitting in the captain's swivel chair, watching the game and sipping Coke out of a can.

Manny explained the crewman. "Mr. Whitfield, he at his place in Palm Springs, not expected for a couple more days. Maybe sooner, maybe longer. I think he looking for a new chick."

"I wish Donny could get away from school and come down here," Cleo said. "We could have a party. Wouldn't that be fun?"

Manny laughed. "Aunts not supposed to like parties. And why you want Donny?"

"You need a lot of people to have a real party and I hardly know any."

"Donny not a real people. He a pig."

"He gives me chocolate bars and imitates Mrs. Holbrook and makes me laugh."

Manny moved his mouth around as if he intended to spit in the ocean. Then he remembered he was below deck and he swallowed instead.

"Besides," Cleo added, "if we were having a party and Mr. Whitfield suddenly appeared, it would be okay because Donny would be here. . . . Don't you think so, Ted?"

Ted didn't even hear the question. He was busy examining the pictures on the wall with the air of a connoisseur.

"Okey doke," Manny said, and showed her how to open the red leather case where the phone was concealed. Then he and Ted went to see the boat's navigation room.

It took about five minutes and considerable lying to reach Donny at Holbrook Hall.

"Hey, Donny, it's me."

"Who's me?"

"Cleo. Guess what. I'm on the *Spindrift*."

"What are you doing there?"

"I'm with Ted. You remember Ted, who picks me up at

school sometimes. He's the one that drives the car you like, the kind your dad's going to buy you if you ever get off probation."

"That'll be in about a million years," Donny said bitterly. "Maybe more."

"Oh, don't be so gloomy. Come on down and we'll celebrate."

"Celebrate what?"

"I'm getting married."

"Why?"

"Because of the baby."

"No kidding, you're going to have a real baby?"

She didn't like the question. "Of course it's real, dumbie. And I'm sailing to Ensenada on my honeymoon. You can come along if you want to."

"Sure I want to. A lot of good that does. You know how they watch me around this joint, like I was public enemy numero uno."

"Dream up something. Like the laundry truck. Remember when you stole the laundry truck?"

"I got caught."

"That was just bad luck, hitting the tree," Cleo said. "Why don't you try again?"

"I'll think about it."

He didn't have to think about it very long. That was the morning Aragon left his car keys in the ignition.

The party had all the elements of success, beginning with the people: Manny Ocho and the crewmen about to visit their families for the first time in weeks, Cleo ready for her honeymoon, Donny, who'd finally escaped from Holbrook Hall and didn't intend to go back—"If dear old dad shows up we'll throw him overboard"—and a footloose young man who'd been kicked out of his house. In addition, the *Spindrift* carried plenty of booze, and one of the crewmen, Velasco, had purchased a quantity of hashish from a lower State Street bar, using money he had collected from the others on board.

The party began with lunch: guacamole prepared by Velasco and served with corn chips, and beluga caviar which Whitfield kept in a supposedly foolproof safe. None of them actually liked caviar but it had such an impressive price they felt duty bound to eat it. Cleo tried to pretend it was black tapioca but Velasco kept talking about "feesh eggs. Nearly three hundred dollars a pound for feesh eggs," and Ted sang a song about virgin sturgeon needing no urging. Ocho sprinkled his share with Tabasco sauce and rolled it up in a tortilla.

When the others had finished eating, Donny scooped up everything that was left on their plates and piled it on his own—guacamole, corn chips, caviar—until it looked like a heap of dog vomit. Eventually he had to go on deck to throw up. Cleo went with him, and being very suggestible, she threw up too.

Then she and Donny sat side by side in the bow, watching the gulls quarreling and listening to the music coming from the cabin, Velasco playing the harmonica and Ted singing dirty fraternity songs. Cleo couldn't make out the words of all the songs because the cabin was tightly closed to prevent the odor of hashish from reaching the wrong noses. Donny was sweating so much his hair was wet and water rolled down from his forehead onto his cheeks like tears.

"Your face is very red," Cleo said.

"What do I care? I can't see it."

"Is my face red?"

"I dunno. I can't see that either."

This was such a hilarious joke that Donny doubled up

with laughter. Cleo wasn't amused. Throwing up had made her feel quite sober.

"Donny," she said. "Do you ever have foggy moments?"

"Foggy? Naw. I get flashes, great big bright white flashes. I see things never been seen before. It's a blast, man."

"Why do you call me man?"

"It's just an expression. Besides, you got no boobs."

"I'm going to grow some when the baby comes."

"Naw. You're built like a man."

"Oh, I am not. Look."

Cleo took off her T-shirt.

"Pimples," Donny said. "Just a couple of pimples."

"Roger liked them."

"He would. He's gay, stupid." Donny looked at her sharply. "Don't tell me you ever made it with that creep."

"Practically. We were even supposed to be married, but suddenly it wasn't such a good idea. I'm going to marry Ted instead."

"When?"

"I don't know. I haven't told him yet."

"Oh, wow. You really are a kook. I thought you were related to him."

"We're only sort of related. Anyway, he was away at school most of the time and I was at home so we hardly knew each other so we're practically strangers. He's the father."

"Father?"

"Of my baby." She giggled. "Me and Ted, we made it, right down the hall from where Hilton was sleeping. Only it turned out he wasn't sleeping. He came charging in and made a horrible fuss."

Donny threw up again over the railing. This seemed to give him extra insight into the situation. "You can't have the kid. There's no such thing as being sort of related. If you and Ted are related, the kid will be even more half-witted than you are."

"I'm not half-witted," Cleo said obstinately. "And I also got boobs."

"You should have an abortion."

"Well, I won't, so there."

"Okay, but don't say I didn't warn you. Wait'll the kid comes out with two heads and one leg. . . . Oh, for Christ's sake, don't start crying. I'm just trying to get you to face facts. If Ted doesn't want to marry you he won't, and you can't force him." Donny had one of his bright white flashes. "Unless he's stoned. That's it. We can get him stoned and drag him to a preacher."

"We don't need a preacher," Cleo said. "I saw this television movie where as soon as the boat left the dock the captain began marrying two people."

"My old man wouldn't go for that. He's against marriage."

"Then how about Manny? Or you?"

"Me?" The idea had instant appeal to Donny but he refused at first to admit it. "I couldn't do that. I'm not the captain."

"You're the owner's son, you could just make yourself the captain. You could proclaim it. You got rights, Donny. As soon as the boat leaves the dock you can say, 'I proclaim myself captain.' "

" 'I proclaim myself captain.' Hey, I like that." Donny stood up straight and assumed a Napoleonic pose. "I proclaim myself captain."

"Aye aye, sir," Cleo said.

The party ended early, with everyone going to bed wherever they lost consciousness. Festivities were resumed the following morning when Ted and Velasco went ashore for fresh supplies. They didn't bother with caviar or more avocados for guacamole; they went directly to the bar on lower State Street where Velasco had purchased the hashish. It was closed, so they made a buy from a man standing outside a pawnshop and then returned to the boat.

Throughout the day Cleo tried to persuade Manny Ocho to cast off without waiting for the arrival of Donny's father. Ocho, who despised Whitfield, would have liked to oblige, but he had too strong a sense of survival. Jobs like his didn't come along very often. Rich men were getting stingier, learning to skipper their own craft and picking up unpaid crews here and there, mostly teenagers and restless young men like Ted who wanted travel and adventure more than wages.

That night Ocho had a telephone call from Palm Springs. Whitfield said he would drive up the next morning, check in at his condo for an hour or so, then come aboard ready to sail.

Ocho broke the news to the others that this was to be the last night of the party. They cheered themselves up by opening a case of Johnny Walker and starting a series of toasts: to the Presidents of the United States and Mexico, the Los Angeles Dodgers, the man who invented scotch, and the *Spindrift*, "the greatest ketch ever caught." This was Ted's contribution.

"When you catch a ketch," he said. "The ketch is caught."

Donny laughed, but neither Cleo nor the three Mexicans understood the pun, even when Ted repeated it with emphasis and gestures.

"When you catch a ketch, the ketch is caught."

"Aw, the hell," Velasco said, and proposed a toast of his own, to Señora Pinkass and her girls of Tijuana.

The final toast was proposed by Ocho to Whitfield, or rather to "his money, which keeps us all afloat."

176

But the party lacked the festive spirit of the previous day and night. The imminent arrival of Whitfield cast a pall over the deck as thick as a summer fog. In addition, the stuff that Ted and Velasco had purchased from the man outside the pawnshop turned out not to be hashish but ordinary marijuana mixed with tea leaves.

They smoked it anyway, of course, and eventually Velasco played his harmonica, though Ted declined to sing. He was pretty confused by this time and wanted to go ashore. But Cleo sat on his lap and Donny brought him another tumbler full of Johnny Walker.

"Come on, Ted," Cleo said. "You'll spoil the party if you don't sing."

"I don't remember the words."

"Sure you do. What about that one, 'Dirty Gertie from Bizerte'?"

"Madame," he said with great dignity, "I am not accepting any requests from the audience."

"Not even from me?"

"And who are you?"

"Me. Cleo."

"Aw, leave him alone," Donny said. "He's got a lousy voice anyway."

Donny remained the soberest of the partygoers. He dreaded meeting his father and trying to explain how he'd gotten away from Holbrook Hall. He might be able to convince him that Mrs. Holbrook had given him special permission to go to Ensenada on the *Spindrift*. But then his father might remember that the school wasn't allowed to do anything like that without an investigation and report by the probation department and a lot of other crap. No, words weren't going to work, none that he'd thought of so far.

At six o'clock Manny Ocho turned on the radio to get the news and the weather report. It was then that Cleo found out about Roger Lennard's death. Roger Lennard, thirty-three, had been found dead, possibly a victim of foul play. A description was given of Lennard's visitor, who had been heard quarreling with him. Cleo knew at once it had to be Hilton and she phoned the police and told them. Then she went back to sit on Ted's lap again.

But there was no lap. Ted had passed out on a couch and was lying on his back with his mouth open, snoring. Cleo listened to him for a few minutes, frowning. She wasn't sure she wanted a husband who snored; it might keep her and the baby awake.

Manny Ocho and the two crewmen watched an old movie on television which Cleo had seen half a dozen times before. She went up to join Donny, who was sitting on the bowsprit, brooding.

"Do you snore, Donny?"

"You ask the stupidest questions. How the hell would I know?"

"You don't have to shout."

"You don't have to listen. Go away and leave me alone."

"I have nowhere to go. Ted's asleep and the others are watching a movie with a lot of cowboys which I don't like in the first place."

It was dark by this time and everything on board was wet, even Cleo's hair. She shivered with cold and sadness.

"Poor Roger," she said. "He wouldn't be dead if it wasn't for me. Does that make me a sort of murderer?"

"You did the poor slob a favor."

"Maybe they'll put me on probation like they did you."

"Lay off, will you? I'm trying to think."

"I hate to be alone."

"You're not alone—you got the baby. So why don't you and the kid go below and have a nice heart-to-heart talk?"

"You can be real nasty, Donny."

"Bug off."

She watched the rest of the movie with Ocho and the crewmen. Then all four of them went to bed after a final nightcap.

Donny sat on the bowsprit for a long time trying to straighten out his head. He feared his father's power but he wanted the same thing for himself. He despised Whitfield's collection of young women, yet he lusted after every one of them. He hated the sound of his father's voice, but he wanted to hear it.

He watched a lone star trying to break through the overcast. When it was no longer visible Donny went below to the captain's cabin and took the phone out of the red leather case and called the house in Palm Springs.

It was eleven o'clock. Donny let the phone ring a dozen times in case his father was drunk or in bed with some chick or asleep.

Eventually Whitfield answered and he didn't sound drunk or sleepy. "Who the hell's this?"

"Donny."

"Donny? What are you doing up so late?"

"I couldn't sleep. Anyway, I wanted to talk to you."

Whitfield was immediately suspicious. "Listen, son. You know the school has a limit on spending money."

"I don't want any money."

"Well, that's a switch. Don't tell me you simply wanted to hear my voice."

This was so close to the truth that Donny couldn't speak for a minute. No sound could get past the sudden lump in his throat.

"Son? What's the matter, son?"

"Nothing."

"How's school going?"

"Fine. I'm even taking stuff like—ah, Latin."

"Latin? That's terrific. *Amo, amas, amat*, right?"

"Listen, Dad, I heard the *Spindrift* is going to Ensenada."

"Now where did you hear—?"

"I'd like to go along. The school will give me special permission because I'm doing so well in my studies like, you know, Latin, I'm working real hard."

"Yes. Well, you realize I'd like to take you, son, but the fact is I've invited other company."

"You wouldn't have to tell them I was your son. I could pretend to be one of the crew."

"You're putting me in a bind, son. I'd certainly like to reward you for your change in attitude and behavior but I honestly can't. This is very special company, if you know what I mean."

"Sure. It's okay."

"Donny, you remember that BMW you wanted me to buy you as soon as you get your driver's license back? I'll get one for you, how about that?"

"Thanks."

"Now Donny, it's obvious that you're disappointed. But be patient. Wait a few more years until you're off probation and you and I will take the *Spindrift* all around the world. Tahiti, Bora Bora, Fiji. How's that for a deal?"

"Screw you," Donny said and hung up. By the time he got off probation he'd be an old man.

He went to bed alone in the captain's quarters. Getting up at dawn the next day he showered and dressed for the new role he was about to assume. The clothes came from his father's mahogany wardrobe.

The white tailored slacks were too small, so he wore his own jeans, threadbare at the knees and seat. The navy-blue blazer didn't come close to buttoning but he put it on anyway. The captain's hat was too large, so he stuffed some toilet tissue in the back to make it fit. Then he opened one of the drawers of the rolltop desk and took out the two guns his father always kept there, a Smith & Wesson .22 and a German Luger. Donny used his limited knowledge of firearms, gained during a short session at a military academy, to make sure the guns were loaded and the safeties in order. Then he dropped the .22 into the pocket of the blazer and tucked the Luger in the waistband of his jeans. Already he felt like a new person, and the image in the mirror beside the wardrobe reaffirmed the feeling. It was a captain who stared back at him, a commander, a leader of men.

He went back to the galley.

Velasco was at the stove, mixing up a batch of *huevos rancheros* in a large iron frying pan. "Hey, Donny. You looking good all dressed up."

"I am your new captain," Donny said.

"By golly, no kidding. You hear that, Gomez? We got a new captain."

Gomez, who had gone back to sleep with his head on the table, was not impressed. Donny kicked him on the butt and Gomez woke up with a moan of pain.

"Salute me, you bastard. Salute your new captain."

"What the hell, by golly," Velasco said. "What you doing, Donny?"

"Call me captain and salute me."

"Maybe later. The eggs, they burn if I don't stir."

"Screw the eggs."

Donny went over and pulled the iron frying pan off the stove and dumped its contents on the floor. The mixture oozed red like a fresh kill.

"Hey, Donny, what the hell, Jesus Christ, what you doing?"

"Salute me, *pachuco.*"

"Not *pachuco*. Last night you and me, all of us, amigos. Amigos forever."

"Forever just ended," Donny said. "You got that?"

"Sure, sure."

"Mix up another batch of eggs and serve them to me in my quarters."

"Okay, Donny."

"You don't say 'okay' to a captain. Say it right, dammit."

"Aye aye, sir."

"That's better."

He went in search of Cleo and found her in one of the guest cabins, lying on a bunk with a blanket pulled up to her chin. The outlines of her thin body could hardly be seen under the blanket, so she appeared to be a severed head.

"Cleo, wake up."

"How can I wake up when I'm not asleep?"

"Then open your eyes."

She opened her eyes and saw Donny looking terribly funny in an oversized hat. "What are you all dressed up like that for?"

"I was thinking over what you said last night, about how I got rights, so I'm proclaiming myself captain."

"That's nice."

"Being as I'm now captain, I can marry you."

"I thought I was going to marry Ted."

"Sure you are. But I'm going to be like the minister as soon as we leave shore."

Cleo threw off the blanket and sat up. "Then this is my wedding day."

"Yeah. You got anything to wear besides those crummy jeans?"

"No."

"Come on and we'll search through my dad's— that is,

my quarters and see if some chick left a fancy robe, you know, something flimsy."

Ted was asleep on the opposite bunk, lying on his stomach with his arms at his sides and his head twisted to one side. His mouth was open and he was making snorting and whistling sounds.

They both watched him for a minute. Then Donny said, "Are you sure you want to marry *that?*"

"I guess so. I mean, he looks better when he's awake."

"Give me your shoelaces."

"Why should I?"

"Follow orders."

"But my shoes are the only decent thing I have on. They're practically new from Drawford's."

"I need the laces to tie his hands in case he wakes up and tries to mutiny." Donny showed her the Luger he had tucked in his waistband and the .22 in his pocket. "There'll be no mutiny on my ship."

"Where did you get those?"

"From my dad's— from *my* quarters."

"Are you going to shoot somebody?"

"Maybe. If I have to."

"Even me?"

"We'll see. Give me your shoelaces."

She took the laces out of her shoes and Donny tied Ted's hands behind his back. At one point Ted's snoring changed pitch and rhythm as if he was about to wake up, but he didn't. Cleo watched in silence, deriving some satisfaction from the fact that Ted didn't look like a bridegroom any more than she looked like a bride.

She followed Donny back to the captain's quarters, where they had breakfast served by a mute and sullen Velasco. The change in Velasco and in Donny made Cleo uneasy.

"Maybe this isn't such a good idea," she said when Velasco had left. "Maybe we don't have all those rights Roger said people had."

"We got rights same as everybody else. Now we have to make plans. You know how to use a gun?"

"Point it at somebody and press the trigger."

"No. First you fix the safety." He gave her the .22 and showed her how to do it. "There. Now you're ready to shoot someone."

"What if I don't really want to?"

"You obey orders. On a ship the captain is God."

"You don't look like God to me. He doesn't wear a hat."

"How do you know? Nobody's ever seen him. Maybe he looks exactly like me, fat as a pig."

"Well, I bet when you pass people on the street they don't say, 'There goes God.' "

"Oh, cut that crap and listen. The crew might try to jump ship or sound an alarm. It's up to you to keep them quiet by holding the gun on them."

"What if they won't keep quiet?"

"You shoot them."

"I don't think I'm going to like that part. I've never shot anyone."

"You won't have to. It's nothing but a threat, see? If they try to pull anything, you shoot a hole in the floor to warn them."

"That might make the boat leak."

"It won't make the boat leak, stupid," Donny said. "Now there's one more thing you got to do. I could have saved us a lot of trouble if I'd decided to take over the ship last night. We'd be far at sea by this time. But I didn't, so here we are, no use crying."

"You can't anyway," Cleo said reasonably. "God never cried."

"Oh, can the God bit and let me think a minute." He

pushed the cap back from his forehead and the toilet paper padding fell out on the floor. His face was very red and all screwed up like a fretful baby's. "Now here's the problem. When my dad drives up from Palm Springs he usually leaves very early to avoid the desert heat, so he may be arriving at his condo any minute. If he should look out the window and see the *Spindrift* missing, he'll call the Coast Guard and they'll send the cutter after us right away. So we have to buy time, an hour at least, more if we can get it."

"I've got an idea. Why don't we wait for him and invite him to come along?"

"You loony, don't you know the first thing he'd do? Send for the cops to take me back to that goddam school. Yes, and you too. You got that? *You too.*"

"I don't want to go back. I want to get married."

"Then cooperate. As soon as he arrives he'll check in at his condo. It's on the beach and you can see it from the bridge through binoculars. I'll stand watch, and the minute he arrives I want you to make a call to the condo. I'll give you the number."

"What am I supposed to say?"

"Tell him that you're Mrs. Holbrook's secretary. Then you ask him to come to Holbrook Hall in order to discuss his son's curriculum."

"Curliculum. What's that mean?"

"Never mind what it means. Just say it right. Cur-ri-cu-lum."

"Curriculum. Okay, then what?"

"Then he goes to the school and I order the crew to cast off."

"What if the crew won't listen to you?"

"They'll listen." Donny patted the Luger in his waist-band and laughed. "We're all amigos, all of us. Amigos forever."

Manny Ocho knocked on the door and entered without waiting for permission. Though he had a well-deserved hangover, he was freshly shaved and uniformed.

"Hey, Donny, what's going on? What you say to my crew? And what you doing wearing your father's clothes?"

"They're my clothes. I'm your new captain. Be ready to cast off when I say the word."

"You don't give me orders."

"I give you orders." Donny took the Luger out of his waistband. "And you obey them."

"You crazy boy, Donny. You mixed up in the *cabeza*."

"Don't bother rolling your eyes at Cleo for help. She's on my side and she has a gun too. How do you like that?"

"It's bad," Manny said. "Very bad."

"So don't make it worse by trying anything funny. You stay down here with Cleo while I go up on the bridge. Cleo will entertain you. She does a great striptease. She has nothing much to show, but she shows it anyway."

"This very bad, Donny."

"I'm not Donny. I'm your captain."

After Donny left, Cleo picked up the .22 from the table and began clicking the safety catch off and on for practice. She forgot about Ocho until he spoke to her in the voice he used to shout orders to his crew:

"Stop that."

Cleo was so surprised by his tone that she almost dropped the gun. "I'm not doing anything."

"Maybe by accident."

"No. Donny showed me how to use it."

"You going to use it?"

"Not really. I mean, I guess not unless Donny wants me to."

"You reaching for big trouble, Cleo," Ocho said. "This Donny, he a bad boy, you a nice little girl. You stay nice, you stay away from him."

"I can't. I want to get married."

"You going to marry *Donny*?"

"No. It's—well, it's like this."

She tried to reconstruct the movie she'd seen where the captain married two people as soon as the boat left the dock. But Ocho kept shaking his head and muttering to himself.

Up on the bridge Donny kept the binoculars focused on his father's condominium on the beach. The binoculars were too heavy to allow continual observation, so he raised them every three or four minutes on the lookout for his father's silver-gray Cadillac. He spotted it shortly before ten o'clock, parked in its slot beside the condo. There was no sign of his father or his companion, if any.

He hurried down to the cabin where Ocho and Cleo had turned on the television set and were watching a children's cartoon, Ocho from the captain's swivel chair, Cleo from the table with the gun in front of her.

Ocho switched off the television set and stood up. "Hey, Donny, you listen to me."

"You got nothing I want to hear," Donny said. "Cleo, make that call now."

"I can't remember the number."

"Jeez, I've told you twice: 9694192. Now have you got it?"

"I guess so."

"You remember what to say?"

"Sure. I'm the secretary and then that business about Donny's curliculum."

"Cur-ri-cu-lum."

"Okay, don't scream. Curriculum."

"You listen now, Donny," Ocho said again. "This Cleo, she a nice little girl, you leave her alone, you put her ashore."

Donny turned to Cleo. "You want to go ashore, kid?"

"No, I don't."

"In fact, you invited me here, didn't you? You phoned Holbrook Hall and told me to come down. We were going to have a party, right?"

"Yes."

"So you're not such a nice little girl after all, are you?"

"I didn't mean any harm, Donny."

"I want Manny clued in on what actually happened. You started the whole damn thing, didn't you?"

"Sort of."

"You hear that, Manny? You're not a hero trying to rescue a poor, innocent girl. She's none of those things: not poor, not innocent, not a girl. She's a rich woman, five years older than I am. So I'm the one you ought to feel sorry for."

"I do," Ocho said. "I feel very sorry for you, Donny."

"Then get ready to cast off. As soon as my father leaves his condo we're moving. *We're moving.*"

Ocho shook his head. "I got my family to think of, my job—"

"You got your own hide to think of first." Donny patted the Luger in his waistband. It was beginning to feel uncomfortable poking into his stomach, so he transferred the gun to his coat pocket. "Look at it this way. It's your hide against my hide and I like my hide better. Isn't that reasonable?"

"Yes, sir."

"And you'll spell it out to the crew?"

"Yes, sir."

Donny returned to the bridge to watch the condo for any further signs of activity. As soon as he saw the silver Cadillac leave its parking slot he called Ocho, and the two of them went to the navigation room.

The engine wouldn't start.

"Good," Ocho said. "Stiff. Not used for a whole month."

"Goddam it, you're supposed to keep the thing ready to go at any time."

"You goddam it yourself. I keep it good. I keep it the best."

"Then start it the best."

On the second attempt the engine turned over, but almost immediately Donny reached out and switched it off.

"The phone's ringing. Answer it."

"What you want me to say?"

"Just answer it."

The call was from the harbormaster's office and they both knew trouble was coming. That it came in the form of Aragon was the only surprise.

"Well, well," Donny said when he jerked open the door and Aragon almost fell into the cabin. "Look who's dropped in, my old pal that leaves his car keys in the ignition."

14

It took a moment for Aragon to regain his balance and somewhat longer for his eyes to adjust after the brilliance of the morning sun. The curtains were closed and the cabin seemed relatively gloomy. Donny Whitfield sat at a rolltop desk with a gun in his hand, and standing near him was a short, wiry-looking Mexican wearing a blue-and-white diagonally striped shirt and a light-blue peaked cap. Aragon assumed this was Manny Ocho who had answered the phone.

He started to address Ocho in Spanish but was immediately interrupted.

"Only English spoken here," Donny said. "Well, nice of you to drop in, pal. Now suppose you drop out."

"Is the girl here?"

"What girl?"

"You know what girl."

"Oh, her. Yeah, sure. She's around someplace trying to find the bridegroom. You walked into a wedding. How's that for luck?"

"The wedding had better be postponed," Aragon said. "I intend to take Cleo back to her family."

"You're going to poop the party, right?"

"Right."

"Uh uh. Wrong . . . Manny, you have your orders. Obey them."

"Please, you wait," Ocho said. "Donny, you listen a minute."

"Hurry up."

Ocho turned to leave, shaking his head. As he passed Aragon he muttered a warning about a gun.

"You can be best man," Donny told Aragon. "Or Cleo might even want to change bridegrooms. You're not bad-looking and at least you aren't related. What's your name?"

"Tom Aragon."

"Cleo Aragon. Hmmmm, sort of a nice ring to it. Not that Cleo's particular. She'd marry any guy that's still breathing. Weird thing is, I never knew she was like that when we were at school together. Maybe it's the sea air." Donny laughed. "How's the sea air affecting you, Aragon?"

"Who's the bridegroom?"

"She calls him Ted."

"You've got to stop this crazy thing, Donny. She's his aunt."

"If that doesn't bother Cleo, why should it bother me?"

"Who's going to perform the ceremony? Did they have the necessary blood tests? Did they take out a license?"

"Details. Screw details."

"And did you know that you're violating the terms of your probation by having a gun?"

"Screw probation," Donny said. "Probation is for land-lubbers. At sea it's only a word."

"What kind of stuff are you on, Donny? What did you take?"

"Nothing. I smoked a little pot last night and had a few drinks, but since then, nothing. Nothing from outside anyway. It's the inside stuff that I'm on. It's all coming from inside. There's some pretty strong stuff in there, man, stronger than anything you can buy on the street."

Aragon believed him. Whatever Donny's body was manufacturing, it seemed as powerful and unpredictable as the animal tranquilizer the kids called angel dust.

He said, "Show me where Cleo is and I'll take her home."

"Home? Where the hell's home for people like Cleo and me? A lousy detention school? Juvenile Hall or the slammer? Where the hell is home?"

"Drop the self-pity kick for a minute and pay attention. I want you and Cleo to come with me, and we'll try to straighten out this whole business. I'll even forget about the gun. I didn't see it."

"You saw it and you better not forget it. That's my best friend. Him and me, we can go anywhere we want to, do anything we want to—"

"Cut the crazy talk, Donny."

"Okay, suppose I buy that crap about you trying to straighten things out for me and Cleo. What then? We get sent back to Holbrook Hall or worse, so the rest of you can live happily ever after."

"I can't perform miracles, Donny."

"No? Well, I won't settle for less."

"Is that your final word?"

"You got it. Come on, we'll go up on deck. There might be someone you want to wave bye-bye to." Donny laughed again. "Or didn't you know we've left the dock?"

"No."

"That's the trouble with you brainy guys—you start concentrating on something so hard you're not aware of an earthquake until a brick hits you on the head. We're under way, man. We're off and running."

"There are a lot of serious charges against you already, Donny. Don't add kidnapping."

"Kidnapping? Nobody forced you to come along. Nobody even invited you. You jumped on board. You know what that makes you? A stowaway. I could file a few charges of my own."

"The punishment for kidnapping can be life imprisonment."

"So? With any luck I'll get the death penalty. Meanwhile you and I are going for a little sail. Come on, we don't want to keep Cleo and the bridegroom waiting."

They went up on deck.

Manny Ocho was at the helm. He had the *Spindrift* going several times faster than the harbor speed limit of five miles an hour, and Aragon knew from the glance Ocho gave him that he was doing it in the hope of attracting the attention of the harbor patrol boat. But there was no sign of Sprague or the boat. The only protest came from a small sloop the *Spindrift* passed in the channel.

"Slow down," a man yelled through a megaphone. "You damn near hit me."

Ocho made an obscene gesture and yelled back, "Report me. Call Sprague."

But the sloop merely rolled and pitched in the *Spin-*

drift's wake, and the harbor patrol boat remained at its mooring in front of the office and the Coast Guard cutter was still tied up at the Navy pier.

Traffic was light. The fishing fleet had departed hours ago and the pleasure boaters seldom went out before the afternoon winds began. Even when the *Spindrift* reached the open sea there wasn't enough wind to take over the job of moving the boat. Donny ordered the sails raised anyway.

Working silently and swiftly, Velasco and Gomez raised the sails and Donny pronounced the boat now ready for the wedding ceremony. It was a picturesque setting, but the bride and groom were missing.

"Cleo," Donny shouted. "Where the hell are you? Time to get married."

Cleo appeared on the starboard deck wearing a white chiffon nightgown she'd found in one of the cabin drawers. The gown was too long and she had to hold it up with her left hand while she carried the .22 in her right. Her hair was combed but she'd forgotten to wash her face and her cheeks were still tear-stained.

"I don't feel like a bride," she told Donny.

"You don't look like one either," Donny said. "Where's Ted?"

"I couldn't get his hands untied. You made the knots too tight."

"Oh for chrissake, can't you do anything right? You don't have to untie them. Cut them with a knife."

"I don't want to cut them. They're my shoelaces. They're practically brand-new."

"All right, all right, you hold the gun on our guest here and I'll go and get Ted."

"Hello, Cleo," Aragon said. "Do you remember me?"

She stared at him, frowning. "No."

"You came to my office not too long ago."

"Why?"

"To ask me about your rights—how to register to vote, for instance. You told me about your brother and his wife and about your counselor, Roger Lennard."

"Poor Roger is dead."

"Yes."

"I mustn't think about that now. I'm supposed to be happy. It's my wedding day."

"No, it isn't, Cleo. There's no one on board qualified to perform the ceremony and you don't have the necessary blood tests or license. And even if you had all these things, the marriage wouldn't be legal anyway because you and Ted are related."

"I won't listen to you," she said. "I think you're a nasty man."

Donny came back with Ted. Ted's hands were free and he was rubbing his wrists where the nylon laces had bitten into his skin. He looked angry and confused and he'd wet his pants.

"What's happening around here? I wake up and my hands are tied. My hands are tied, for chrissake. What for? I thought we were having a party."

"That party's over," Donny said. "We're about to start another one. Cleo has decided she wants to get married, and since she's a little short of bridegrooms since Roger died, she picked you."

"Me? For chrissake, why would she pick me?"

"Because she says you're the father of her baby."

"That's impossible. There isn't any baby."

"Oh, Ted, there is so," Cleo said reproachfully. "It's still very tiny, maybe like sort of a grain of sugar or a grape seed."

"There isn't any baby, dammit. We had only started to make love when my father barged in. I didn't even penetrate. You're still a virgin."

"Ted, you know that's not true. We were doing it

exactly like in the movies, no clothes and everything. So now we have to get married."

Ted appealed to Aragon. "Whoever you are, they're both crazy. We have to get out of here."

"Stay cool, and play along," Aragon said quietly. "That's our only chance."

"Why should I marry some half-wit because she thinks she's pregnant? Whatever happened—and God knows it wasn't much—happened just a few days ago. I tell you, she's still a virgin. And even if she weren't she'd have no way of knowing so soon that she was pregnant."

Cleo was crying again. She cried as easily as a plastic doll with a water-filled syringe in her head. "He doesn't want to marry me, Donny. What should I do now?"

"Ask him again, real sweet and polite."

"Nobody wants to marry me."

"Maybe he'll change his mind." Donny pointed the Luger directly at Ted's chest. "Go on, ask him again, Cleo."

"Ted, will you marry me?"

"No. Get it through your thick head, we didn't have complete intercourse. You are not pregnant. You're still a virgin."

"But we had all our clothes off and everything exactly like the movies."

"You're crazy," Ted screamed. "The whole damn bunch of you are crazy."

The first bullet from the Luger grazed his right shoulder. He turned and ran toward the railing. As he jumped overboard a second bullet struck him on the left arm.

Two more struck the water at the same time that Ted did. Cleo began screaming with excitement and jumping up and down until she tripped on the hem of the white nightgown that was her bridal costume. The .22 fell out of her hand and slid across the deck in Aragon's direction.

"Don't move," Donny told Aragon. "It's a bad year for heroes." And to Ocho, who was turning the boat around and heading back toward Ted, "Keep on course. Let the bastard drown."

"Throw him a life jacket," Aragon said.

"Why? A dip in the ocean will cool him off. Maybe he'll have a change of heart and decide Cleo isn't so bad after all."

"He might be seriously injured. And if there are any sharks in the area, the blood will attract them."

"I bet those sharks would be pleasantly surprised to find two guys instead of one," Donny said. "Suppose you go in after him, amigo."

"We're at least a mile from shore. I can't swim very well."

"Learn by experience. That's what they're always telling us at school—learn by experience."

"Give us a sporting chance," Aragon said. "We need two life jackets."

Donny took two life jackets from a forward hatch and threw them at Aragon. After removing his shoes and pants Aragon put one of the life jackets on over his shirt. Then, holding the other jacket in his hand, he jumped into the water.

Ted was some hundred yards from the boat, not yelling for help or trying to swim. His eyes were closed and Aragon thought he was unconscious until he saw that Ted's legs were moving slightly to keep him from rolling over on his stomach.

The water temperature at this distance from shore and beyond the thick kelp beds that paralleled the coast was still well below sixty degrees. This might be low enough to slow the bleeding of Ted's arm and help numb his pain. But it might also be low enough to cause both men to suffer from exposure unless they were picked up within an hour or so. Even without the complication of Ted's wounds, hypothermia could be fatal without quick treatment.

The *Spindrift* was turning away, its engine accelerating as it headed southwest. Watching it pull away, Aragon had a moment of panic. He knew he would be unable to drag Ted over the kelp beds and in to shore, and their only hope was to be spotted by a passing boat or one of the low-flying helicopters that serviced the oil platforms.

Both were possible. The sea was calm, with a long smooth swell and no whitecaps to hide any floating object.

This was Aragon's first attempt to swim while wearing a life jacket and he found it difficult to move his arms. He rolled over on his back and used his legs as propellants.

He shouted, "Ted, can you hear me?"

Ted opened his eyes. He looked dazed and terrified. "Shot me—arm—"

"I want you to help me get this life jacket on you."

Ted kept saying, "Shot me—shot me—" as if he was more overcome by surprise than by a sense of danger or by pain.

"Put your injured arm through here first. Then I'll pull the jacket around your back and get the other arm through. It may hurt but it has to be done."

"Shot me—shot me—"

"Stop that. You have to cooperate. Understand?"

It took several minutes for the life jacket to be put on and fastened. Ted was gradually becoming more rational and more aware of the danger they were in. He asked about the *Spindrift*.

"It's gone," Aragon said. "Move your right arm and your legs as much as possible to keep your blood circulating."

"Didn't know—had any left."

"You have lots left." He wasn't sure whether this was true or even whether he'd given the correct advice to Ted to keep moving. He only knew that the water was incredibly cold. His original estimate of being able to survive an hour or two without much damage now seemed ridiculous. He was already numb below the ankles and suffering from what was called in his boyhood an ice-cream headache. He'd never taken a lifesaving course or even one in first aid, and he wished now he had paid more attention to some of his wife's lectures on practical medicine.

Ted said, "You shot?"

"No."

"'What are you doing here?"

"I wanted to cool off."

"You got it."

A great blue heron flew overhead, his neck folded, his long legs stretched out stiffly behind him like a defeathered tail.

Ted had closed his eyes again and the wind was picking up. These were both bad omens. The rougher the sea, the more difficult it would be for anyone to spot them, and the greater the chances of Ted choking on salt water.

"Ted, keep moving."

"Can't— Tired."

"A boat will come along any minute."

"Tired. Leave me alone."

Ted's youth was a plus factor. But there were too many minuses. Before he was shot he'd spoken of a party on board, and it was obvious then that he was suffering a hangover from alcohol or drugs or both. Also, he probably hadn't eaten in many hours and his resistance was lowered.

"A boat will come along any minute," Aragon repeated. "We'll be rescued. Do you hear me, Ted?"

If Ted heard, he didn't believe it or didn't care enough to open his eyes.

"Are you listening, Ted? By this time Whitfield will have gone back to the harbor and found his boat missing.

He'll send the Coast Guard out after it right away. They should be passing us any minute. Hear that, Ted? Any minute. Hang on. Don't give up, Ted. Move. Try harder. Move."

He kept saying the same things over and over like a coach peptalking one of his players during a game.

The wind was still rising, and now and then his voice was choked off as a wave slapped his face. The increase in wind velocity would have the effect of luring the Lasers and Mercuries and Lidos and Victories, the Hobie Cats and Alpha Cats and Nacras. But these smaller craft usually stayed inside the kelp line. The larger craft, like the fishing fleet, had departed much earlier in the day, going out under power, some as far as the Island twenty-five miles offshore, to return in the afternoon under sail.

Aragon continued talking, using both his hands to hold Ted's head as far out of the water as possible. The numbness had spread through his whole body and he was feeling hardly any discomfort. He remembered reading that people who froze to death didn't suffer pain the way people did who burned to death.

He heard his own voice coaxing, ordering, questioning, demanding, and he wondered if it was all being wasted on a dead man.

"Cut it out, Ted. Now open your eyes. You've got to cooperate. Get in there and pitch. Keep kicking your legs. We're going to be rescued. Any minute. Any minute. You hear? Open your eyes, dammit, open your eyes."

But his voice was getting weaker and the numbness seemed to have reached his brain like a dose of Pentothal. When he finally heard the engine he was only mildly interested, and the men yelling at him seemed to be making a fuss over nothing. One of them had orange hair and looked a little like some woman, someone he'd known a long time ago. A long long time ago . . .

* * *

The orange hair emerged from the fog like a sunrise. It had a face in the middle, not a young face or a pretty one, but familiar and reassuring.

"You really blew it this time, junior," Charity Nelson said. "I brought you some carnations. That's how I know you're awake. I put one under your nose and your nostrils twitched."

He struggled to speak. His voice sounded as if it were coming from under water. "How—Ted?"

"Hush. The doctor told me not to let you talk when you woke up. How's Ted Jasper? Still alive in the Intensive Care Unit and his mother's with him. That's all I know."

He turned his head to one side and saw the cot beside the window, looking as if it had been slept in.

"Your doctor's been with you all night," Charity said. "I sent her out to get some breakfast. How are you feeling?"

"All right."

"Smedler gave me the whole day off to help look after you. I was a nurse once. I don't remember much about it but I can still plump pillows, give a bath and hold your hand. Want me to hold your hand?"

"More than I want you to give me a bath."

"I'll overlook that remark, junior. Are you hungry? Of course you are. How about something revolting like poached eggs and mashed potatoes? You're supposed to be on a soft diet."

"Why?"

"Beats me. If I were in charge of your case I'd give you steak and french fries. There's nothing like a long cold swim to sharpen the appetite." Charity leaned over and peered into his face. "Everything considered, you don't look so bad. Maybe your doctor will let you have steak and french fries after all. She's very sympathetic. Cute, too. In fact, a real knockout, with blue eyes and black hair and dimples. Dimples yet. I've always wanted dimples. When I was in high school I sent away for something advertised in *True Romances* guaranteed to make dimples. For one buck I received a little piece of metal I was supposed to stick in my cheek with adhesive plaster every night. I used it and in the morning I'd have a dimple for fifteen minutes. That's the story of my life—none of my dimples lasted more than fifteen minutes."

"Laurie," he said. "You were describing my wife, Laurie."

"Of course I was. I called her yesterday afternoon as soon as I heard what had happened. Smedler himself went to pick her up at the airport. How's that for a first?"

"Laurie." He put his arm over his forehead so Charity wouldn't see the tears welling in his eyes.

She saw them anyway. "Now don't get sloppy and sentimental. Here's some Kleenex. Or maybe you'll need a towel if you're going to pull out all the stops. Incidentally she seems crazy about you too. She doesn't see as much of you as I do—that may explain why."

He wiped his eyes with the piece of Kleenex she handed him. "Who rescued—?"

"Don't ask questions and I'll tell you what I know. The harbormaster became suspicious when you didn't come back from the *Spindrift*. He tried to contact the boat by phone and couldn't. Then he saw it speeding out of the harbor and he notified the Coast Guard. They sent the cutter after you. Ted Jasper was in bad shape by that time, suffering from loss of blood and shock and hypothermia. You had some degree of hypothermia but they warmed you up and stuck a few needles into you and here you are."

"What about Cleo and Donny?"

"They've both been arrested. That's all I was able to find out."

Donny Whitfield. He thought of the fat, morose boy

he'd first seen outside Holbrook Hall. If it wasn't for one small mistake, Donny might still be there, sitting under the oak tree eating corn chips and chocolates. *It's my fault. I made the mistake. I left the keys in the ignition. My fault—*

"My fault," he said and began shaking his head back and forth as if to shake off his guilt.

"Stop that," Charity said, readjusting the oxygen mask none too gently. "Any more acting up and I'll call the nurse to jab you with another needle."

"Car key—"

"What do you want your car keys for? You're not going anyplace. Now shut up or I'll resign from your case. This Florence Nightingale bit is a drag. Where do you want me to put the flowers I brought you?"

He told her.

"Junior, that's not nice. But since irritability is one of the first signs of convalescence, I'll overlook it this time. I may, however, bring it up in the future when you're asking for a favor at the office. By the way, congratulations."

"What for?"

"You were hired to find Cleo. You found her."

There was a knock on the door. Charity said, "Come in. . . . Oh, he's doing fine. Weepy, hungry, crabby. Can't ask for better signs."

"Thank you, Miss Nelson."

The voice was pleasant and cool; the hand that touched his forehead was soft, the fingers on his pulse gentle.

"I'm Dr. MacGregar," she said. "I'm in charge of your case and I don't believe you need that oxygen mask on anymore. Mind if I remove it?"

"Laurie. *Laurie.* It's really you."

"Please don't get emotional—Tom, you might have died. You might have *died.*"

They held each other close for a long time, unaware that Charity was watching from the doorway. She would be expected to describe the scene later to all the girls in the office and she wanted to make sure she didn't miss any details.

Rachel Holbrook knew what was coming but she was not sure when or what form it would take: perhaps an invitation to appear at the next board of directors meeting in two or three weeks, or a formal letter from the executive committee, or a long-winded legal document full of whereases and therefores. What she didn't expect was a phone call from Smedler, her only longtime friend among the directors.

Smedler didn't waste time on amenities. "Have you seen today's papers, Rachel?"

"No."

"The reporters and photographers are having a field day with this. The L.A. *Times* has it featured as their leading story, and in the local paper there's a whole page of pictures, a rundown on everyone involved and even a history of the school. There'll undoubtedly be an editorial within the next few days crying for blood. Some of it is bound to be yours, Rachel."

"That's understandable."

"For sure they'll demand an investigation of the school and its policies. There'll be suggestions ranging from your resignation to the complete closure of the school, all from outraged citizens, many of whom have wanted to close the place for years."

"What do you propose that I do?"

"Anticipate. Get your licks in first and fast. Write a letter requesting an indefinite leave of absence until the matter has been fully investigated and steps are taken to prevent further incidents."

"Indefinite," she said. "That could mean a long time."

"Yes."

"I can't be held responsible for what happened."

"Whether you can be or can't be, you will be. Harsh criticism is inevitable, perhaps a drop in enrollment and some defections among the faculty. There may also be a decrease in donations and bequests. You're in for a lot of flak, Rachel. The only way you can avoid it is by leaving town for a while."

"Perhaps I should change my name and assume a disguise."

"Don't be bitter, Rachel. This thing has affected a great number of people. Some of them will want your hide. So put it out of reach. Take a holiday."

"Is that your legal advice?"

"It's my advice as a friend. I hope it will be accepted in the same spirit."

"Thanks. I'll think about it."

"Pack first, think later," Smedler said. "There's only one hitch to the plan. Should the police ask you to stick around, you'll have to stick. You may be subpoenaed if and when the Whitfield boy comes to trial and there's some kind of hearing concerning Cleo. But if I were you, right now I'd sit down and write a letter requesting an indefinite leave of absence. Bring it to my office and I'll have copies made and hand-delivered to all the members of the board. Your request will be immediately accepted."

"Thanks for your advice."

"Honestly, Rachel, you don't know how much I hate to do this to you."

"Not as much as I hate to have it done."

She hung up and reached for a sheet of the school's best stationery.

I hereby request an indefinite leave of absence from my duties as principal of Holbrook Hall.

204

She signed her name, put the sheet of paper in an envelope and addressed the envelope to the president of the board of directors. Then she went outside by the back door.

Nothing seemed to have changed. There were the usual sounds: screams and laughter from the pool area, the whinnying of a horse, the excited barking of dogs.

Gretchen was polishing the leaves of a camellia planted in a redwood tub. Only such sturdy leaves as a camellia's could have withstood her loving attack.

"Good morning, Gretchen. I see you're working hard."

"I always do," Gretchen said brusquely, as if she'd been accused of laziness. "*Somebody* has to."

The fig tree was dropping its fruit like small brown eggs onto the grass. As they fell, two boys wearing cowboy boots were squashing the eggs into little yellow omelettes.

The round-eyed girl, Sandy, was shelling peanuts to feed to the scrub jay watching impatiently from the edge of the roof. Sandy would place a peanut on her head and the bird would swoop down, grab it with his beak and fly off to hide it. There were pounds and pounds of nuts scattered throughout the grounds, buried in the grass or the vegetable garden, stuffed in the crevices between flagstones and the hollows of trees and underneath the shingles of the roof, dropped into chimneys and even into the goldfish pond. The bird always tired of the game before the girl did and flew off to seek more challenging pastimes.

In the playground the quiet boy, Michael, sat in the middle of the teeter-totter, using his feet to pump it up and down. Bang thump. Bang thump. He wore a knitted headband which had fallen or been pulled down over his eyes.

"Michael, I'm going away. I wanted to say goodbye to you. I probably won't be seeing you for a long time."

Bang thump. Bang thump.

"Michael?"

"I hate you."

"I know you do. I thought you might say goodbye to me anyway."

"Goodbye," Michael said. "Goodbye. Goodbye. Goodbye. Goodbye. Goodbye. Goodbye."

"Thank you, Michael. That's enough."

"Goodbye. Goodbye. Goodbye."

She walked away as fast as possible. But she couldn't get out of earshot. The others had taken up Michael's chant. Sandy and the two boys under the fig tree and Gretchen were all chanting in unison with Michael.

"Good . . . bye . . . good . . . bye . . . good . . ."

When she reached the corner of the building Rachel Holbrook turned and waved. They waved back, Gretchen and the two boys and Sandy and even Michael. It was an encouraging sign that Michael had responded at all. Perhaps as he grew older, under the guidance of a new principal . . . *No, I really mustn't think about any of them. I must go away and forget them for a long time. . . .*

"Goodbye," she said firmly.

The room was small and bare except for three steel chairs and a table, all bolted to the floor. The door had a barred window through which a uniformed policeman glanced every few minutes.

A previous occupant had damaged the thermostat and the air-conditioning couldn't be regulated. Cold air kept blasting in from a vent high in the wall, making the room as cold as a walk-in refrigerator. Donny sat on the table dangling his legs.

"How about that," he said, gesturing toward the door. "My own personal guard. Man oh man, they must think I'm public enemy numero uno. Did you bring me any money?"

Whitfield shook his head. "They wouldn't let me hand you any, so I tried to deposit some in an account at the commissary. But they don't have that system at Juvenile Hall, just at the adult—ah, facility."

"So what system are us poor jerks in here stuck with?"

"You have to earn points."

"How?"

"Good behavior, doing work, et cetera. You earn so many points by doing such and such a job and then you can spend the points like money. If you work and behave yourself you'll be able to get candy bars and cigarettes, things like that. The idea is to treat rich and poor alike."

"Jee—sus."

"Well, godammit, son, this isn't a hotel. And I didn't put you here."

"You sent the cops after your precious boat."

"I didn't," Whitfield said. "I swear I didn't. I would have let you take a little cruise, knowing you'd come back."

"So you think I'd come back. Don't kid yourself. I was heading for the moon, man, straight for the moon."

Whitfield focused his eyes on a spot on the bare gray wall. This was his son, his only child, and he couldn't bear to look at him, to touch him, even to be in the same room with him. "I didn't put you here, Donny."

"But I bet you don't mind if they keep me here. It's cheaper than Holbrook Hall."

"Listen, son. I've hired a lawyer from L.A., the best money can buy. But he can't get you out on bail. There's no bail for juveniles, especially ones with a record like yours. And the charges against you are pretty bad."

"Like how bad?"

"I don't even know if I can remember them all. Kidnapping—that's the worst. Then there's grand theft, assault with a deadly weapon, assault with intent to do great bodily harm, assault with intent to commit murder—"

"Okay, okay."

"Although you were brought here to Juvenile Hall because you're not yet eighteen, the chances are ninety-nine to a hundred that you'll be tried as an adult. That makes things even worse." The room was so cold that Whitfield's voice was trembling. "Donny, if you could only show remorse, if you could convey to the authorities that you're sorry for what you've done, that you didn't mean to—"

"I meant to," Donny said. "And I'm not sorry."

"Son, please."

"Screw the son bit. It makes me puke. . . . You got any chocolate bars on you?"

"I brought you two pounds of See's candies but they wouldn't let me bring them in."

"Those stinking cops are probably gobbling them up right now." Donny slid off the table. He looked impassive except for a tic in his left eyelid which he concealed by averting his face. "Well, I guess that's all. You might as well leave. You'll be late getting to Ensenada."

Whitfield once more studied an invisible spot on the wall. "I was going to cancel the trip to make sure I'd be here for your trial. But the lawyer told me not to bother. He said there'd probably be one delay after another, so your case might not come up for as long as a year, and it would be a waste of time for me to wait around and. . . ." His voice faded as if suddenly he knew he'd hit the wrong note but there was no right one. "I'm sorry. I'm doing everything I can, everything I possibly can."

"Yeah. Sure."

"Donny. Donny, couldn't you at least *pretend* to be remorseful?"

"I'm remorseful all right when I think of those damn cops gobbling up all my candies. What kind were they?

Any marshmints? Chocolate cherries? Peanut butter crackle?"

"For God's sake, Donny, haven't you anything else to say to me?"

"Marshmints are my favorites," Donny said.

Cleo was still wearing the stained jeans and T-shirt and sneakers without laces when Hilton went to the county jail to take her home.

Bail had been set high, at twenty-five thousand dollars, because she would be charged as a principal in the case, which one of the lawyers said was the new term used for accessory to a crime. Hilton tried to explain this to her on the way home.

"You will be accused of helping Donny do some of the things he's charged with. Do you understand?"

"All I did was hold the gun."

"Did he force you to? Were you acting under duress?"

"It was hardly even a gun. It was only an itty-bitty thing."

"Guns kill. That's what they're made for. Did you obey Donny because you were afraid for your life?"

"Heavens, no. Who could be afraid of Donny? He's so silly."

She sat beside him in the front seat, her legs drawn up and her chin resting on her knees. Her face was almost hidden by a beige curtain of hair.

"Where are your shoelaces?" he said.

She told him about Donny tying Ted's hands behind his back as he lay on the bunk. Hilton listened, feeling the blood flow out of him as if each word she spoke was a puncture wound in his heart.

He ached with fatigue. He had been up all night, contacting lawyers, the judge who set bail, a medical doctor and a psychiatrist recommended by a bail bondsman.

Every half hour he phoned the hospital for a report on Ted's condition. He knew that whether Ted lived or died, Frieda would hold him responsible. His marriage had ended and his son was listed in very critical condition, yet he still knew almost nothing of what had happened since Cleo had walked away from the house with the basset hound on a leash. The psychiatrist had urged him not to question Cleo too closely. What good would it do anyway? A gun was an itty-bitty thing and Donny was merely silly.

"There was a nasty old doctor at the jail," Cleo said. "He told me I'm not going to have a baby. How does *he* know anyway? He can't see it if it's no bigger than a grain of sugar."

"It's his job to know. He's a gynecologist."

"Long words don't mean anything. Curriculum. Curriculum—what is that anyway? Donny had one at the school. ... Will I be going back there, to Holbrook Hall?"

"I don't think so."

"Oh, well, I don't care. It wasn't all that much fun." She hesitated. "Will I be staying at home all the time like I used to?"

"That depends."

"What on?"

"The judge will have to decide to what extent you were responsible for your actions."

"I didn't do anything wrong, Hilton. I just held that little wee gun."

"Stop it. I prefer not to hear any more about it."

"Oh, Hilton, you're mad at me." She peeked at him around the curtain of hair, wet-eyed and wistful. "Aren't you?"

"No."

"I'm glad. I didn't really do anything much."

His hands gripped the steering wheel as if they were trying to squeeze the life out of it. Nothing much. Roger

Lennard was dead and Ted on the point of death. Rachel Holbrook's lifework was in ruins and Donny Whitfield would almost certainly be sent to the penitentiary. Nothing much.

"Everything can be the same as it was before," Cleo said. "Frieda will read to me, and we'll go shopping and to the movies, and maybe Frieda will teach me how to drive. Roger said that was one of my rights, to learn to drive."

"Frieda won't be living with us anymore."

"Why not?"

"She doesn't want to."

The simple explanation satisfied her because she understood it. If you wanted to do something, you did it. If you didn't, you didn't.

"You can hire somebody to take her place, can't you?" Cleo said. "Somebody like her, only nicer and more understanding."

"I'm afraid I couldn't find such a person."

"That means there'll just be the two of us, you and me? It doesn't sound like much fun."

"No, I don't suppose it will be."

"Valencia hardly speaks any English and Cook always chases me out of the kitchen because I interfere with the TV game shows. I won't have anyone to talk to unless you stay home."

"I can't, Cleo. I have a job."

"We have lots of money already, don't we?"

"Quite a bit, yes."

"Why do you want more?"

"To provide for your future. You're only twenty-two. You may live another fifty or sixty years. You'll require a great deal of money."

"No, I won't, Hilton. I'll have a husband to take care of me. Won't I?"

He didn't answer.

211

"Won't I, Hilton? Won't I have a husband?"

"I don't know."

"I bet you don't want me to. I bet you're jealous. Look what you did to Roger."

"You mustn't talk like that, Cleo. There's nothing in this world I'd like better than to see you married to a decent young man who will love you for your—your good qualities."

"I don't believe it. You told me I was never to let another man touch me. Don't you remember, it was the night Ted and I—"

"I spoke during an emotional reaction. I didn't mean it. After you're married you will have an intimate relationship with your husband like any other girl."

"But I'm not like any other girl, am I?"

"No."

"I wonder why not."

He turned into the long, winding driveway that led to the house. About halfway up, Trocadero was putting the finishing touches on a juniper sculpture, cutting the tiny needles as precisely as a barber. The basset hound Zia sat at his feet but came bounding out to bark at the car. Troc whistled him back and pretended not to see Cleo.

"Zia doesn't like me anymore," Cleo said. "I can tell. He wasn't even wagging his tail."

"We'll buy you a dog of your own, any kind you like."

"No thanks."

"Don't you want one?"

"I'd rather have a husband and babies."

"Of course you would. But in the meantime—"

He couldn't finish the sentence. It would be a long meantime, impossible to fill with dogs and movies and shopping.

He stopped the car in front of the house. "You'd better

go up to your room and take a shower and put on some clean clothes."

"I don't want to. I like these ones."

"They're dirty. Valencia will wash and dry them for you while we're having lunch. Please don't argue with me, Cleo. I'm terribly tired."

"I'm just as tired as you are. The jail was so noisy I couldn't sleep."

"Then we'll both take a long nap after lunch. Right now I have to call the hospital again."

She went up to her room and showered and shampooed her hair. Then she stood in front of the full-length mirror in her bedroom, letting the water drip down her body, tickling her skin. She liked the way she looked, a mermaid escaped from the sea.

Valencia came in without knocking to pick up Cleo's clothes and take the wet towels away.

Valencia said, *"Hija mala."*

"You're mean to say things I can't understand."

"Wicked girl. You done wicked."

"No, I didn't."

"Troc say you wicked. Cook say you loco."

"What do they know? They're only servants."

She put on one of the bathrobes Frieda had given her and went downstairs to have lunch with Hilton. But he was lying on the couch in his den, his face to the wall. She wondered if he was dead, so she touched him on the shoulder. It was like switching on one of the mixing machines Cook kept in the kitchen. Hilton began to shake all over as if he were being ground up inside, his liver and heart and stomach and appendix, all ground up into hamburger. It took away her appetite.

She went into the kitchen to see if Cook would let her watch television with her. But Cook shooed her away like a chicken, flapping her apron at her and making chicken sounds. So she sat at the long dining room table by herself, thinking about Hilton's insides being all ground up. She left most of the food on her plate untouched and ate only a muffin. Then she went back into the den.

"Hilton?"

"Go away."

"I have nowhere to go."

He was still shaking but not nearly so much, and his voice had no tremor at all. He just sounded very tired.

"Ted died," he said. "The bullet taken out of him was a twenty-two. It came from your gun."

"I don't believe it. You're trying to scare me."

"You shot him. You shot my son, Ted."

"Honestly I didn't. I only held the gun. I only held that teeny little gun. You can't blame me."

"I don't blame you. I blame myself."

"That's silly. You weren't even there."

"Go away," Hilton said. "Go away."

She returned to her room, thinking that Hilton's brain, not merely his liver and stomach and heart, had been ground up in the mixer because he was imagining that Ted had died and that he himself was to blame. It was too bad. Hilton used to be awfully smart.

She brushed her hair, still wet, and put on the freshly laundered jeans and T-shirt, and wondered where mermaids went when they came up from the sea. There didn't seem to be a place for them.

She asked Valencia, who didn't understand the word, and Cook, who said, "Never you mind about mermaid. March back in there and finish your vegetables."

Then she walked down to where Troc was barbering the juniper and she asked him about mermaids.

Troc gave her a peculiar look. "Are you having one of them foggy moments of yours?"

"All I did was ask you a question."

"I'll go fetch the boss. You wait here, girl. You wait right here."

She waited only long enough for him to disappear around the bend. Then she ran down the rest of the driveway to the street. She felt very light and airy, moving with the wind like a silk sail. And suddenly, magically, she knew what mermaids did when they came up from the sea. They went down to it again.

She could see the harbor in the distance and she kept running toward it. Everyone on the *Spindrift* would be very surprised to see her and they would all have a party to celebrate, Manny Ocho and the crew, and Donny and Ted and the young man who told her about voting and some of her other rights.

None of that seemed important anymore. She was going to a party.